C000203310

A MURDER IN LONG ISLAND

PENELOPE BANKS MURDER MYSTERIES

COLETTE CLARK

DESCRIPTION

A death in a locked room and a house full of suspects....
New York, 1925

Penelope "Pen" Banks has a knack for puzzling things out and the uncanny ability to remember everything she sees. Two talents that have helped her make ends meet playing cards in clubs and speakeasies. Now, they might just help her discover the true cause of death for a dear old family friend.

Agnes Sterling, has been found dead in her Long Island home. The official cause of death is ruled a suicide. After all, she was found in her locked bedroom with both the bottle of poison and a final handwritten note on the bed next to her.

Penelope is certain Agnes Sterling's death was not by her own hand. She's been summoned to Long Island for the reading of the will along with the other beneficiaries. While there, she plans on doing a little sleuthing to discover what really happened to Agnes.

The surprising terms of the will and a secret letter have Pen all the more certain that foul play was at hand.

A Murder in Long Island is the first book in the Penelope Banks Murder Mysteries set in 1920s New York, with a spirited heroine, witty banter, and twists and turns that will leave you guessing. Perfect for readers who enjoy the feel of a cozy mystery with the excitement and daring of Prohibition and the Jazz Age.

ABOUT THE AUTHOR

Colette Clark lives in New York and has always enjoyed learning more about the history of her amazing city. She decided to combine that curiosity and love of learning with her addiction to reading and watching mysteries. Her first series, **Penelope Banks Murder Mysteries** is the result of those passions. When she's not writing she can be found doing Sudoku puzzles, drawing, eating tacos, visiting museums dedicated to unusual/weird/wacky things, and, of course, reading mysteries by other great authors.

Join my Newsletter to receive news about New Releases and Sales!
https://dashboard.mailerlite.com/forms/148684/72678356487767318/share

CHAPTER ONE

MANHATTAN 1925

"You're killin' me, lady."

"I guess I'm just lucky," Penelope "Pen" Banks said with a shrug.

The gentleman sitting across from her certainly didn't like that explanation, especially when she hastily swiped the money from the table.

"That's the fifth time in a row you've won! Something ain't right here."

"You do make a good point, it's well past my bedtime," Penelope Banks announced, noting that her mark was catching on. "It's been fun playing cards with you Mr...."

She realized she had never gotten his last name so she left it at that as she shot up from the chair at the table toward the back of the club, grabbing her bag and coat as she did.

"Now you wait just a—*hey*, stop that broad!"

Penelope hadn't stolen the money, she'd won it fair and square. Mostly. The same peculiar affliction that allowed her to remember everything she saw also came in handy while playing cards, especially with games like 21 or poker.

She could predict with uncanny accuracy what card was likely to show up in a deck.

Some might have called it playing dirty. Penelope called it a blessing. That night had been especially fruitful. She'd made more than she would in a month of working as a book-keeper for that stingy old Mr. Brown, and she'd certainly had a lot more fun doing it.

After tucking the money into her pouch bag, Penelope decided to cut across the dance floor, or at least as much as she could considering how packed the place still was. An upbeat jazz piano tune filled the air. It had everyone performing drunken, uncoordinated variations of the Shimmy and the Charleston, which were easy enough to feign no matter how zozzled you were.

She silently thanked George, the piano player for keeping the crowd going with such an energetic rhythm. At this time of the night, half the floor might as well have been in one of those dance marathons that were so popular these days. How they were still going was beyond her, but it was Friday so most of them had no reason to head home at a decent hour. For now, they provided a decent enough blockade to help a girl out. She made it to the hallway leading behind the stage, which offered a short reprieve.

"I told you not to mess with that man, Pen," scolded Lucille "Lulu" Simmons, the jazz singer and main act of the evening here at the Peacock Club. She was on break, looking divine as usual in a white silk dress that contrasted perfectly against her brown skin.

"You couldn't possibly help me out of this mess, could you?" Penelope asked as she shrugged into her winter coat and put her gloves back on.

It wouldn't be the first time Lulu had helped her out. They had first met when she caught Penelope continuously outwitting a man playing three-card monte. She had seen how eerily observant the young woman was and suggested Pen lend her abilities to more profitable endeavors.

The small cut of the winnings Pen paid to Lulu was worth it. She helped Penelope navigate the unsavory terrain of the Manhattan underworld filled with speakeasies, illegal gambling, and worse. Lulu also knew which clientele had the fattest pockets and a weakness for cards...and which clientele to stay away from, no matter how lucrative the winnings might be.

It had now been three years since Penelope's fall from grace, or rather her fall from the mansions of 5th Avenue. Since that time, Pen had become cozy with all manner of people who would have had no place in her former life.

"I think she went behind the stage!"

The sound of her mark's voice forced Pen's eyebrows together in pleading consternation.

"Go on out the back way." Lucille smiled and jerked her head toward the end of the hallway. "My boys'll take care of you."

"Thanks, Lulu, you're the berries."

Pen rushed along past the dressing rooms and back offices. Behind her a perfect babel filled the air as Lucille's "boys" in the jazz band, also on a break, did their best to block the way of the man she had just relieved of a full hundred clams.

"Get out of my way!"

"Oh, I'm sorry, mister."

"Move that damn horn!"

"My humblest apologies, sir."

"Hey now, what's the idea? I think you're deliberately trying to—"

Penelope couldn't help a soft laugh as she exited

through the back door into the frigid mid-January night. She secured her cloche hat over her brunette bob to fight the instant chill that hit her. The alley behind the Harlem club was no place for a young woman on her own, but she couldn't exactly afford to play the good girl right now. Fortunately, it was empty and she quickly made her way toward the street before tonight's mark got hep to Lucille's little decoy.

"Well now, you look like a bona fide damsel in distress."

As if she wasn't in enough danger.

Tommy Callahan, green-eyed devil and all-around trouble was standing at the curb, smoking the last of a cigarette. His jade irises twinkled with mischievous curiosity as he blew smoke her way. What he was doing near the back alley of a nightclub was something she certainly wasn't going to ask about, but she figured it was nothing legal. Still, beggars couldn't be choosy.

"Damsel in distress indeed. You wouldn't happen to have a noble steed handy would you? Preferably a fast one?"

He grinned and flicked his cigarette away. "It just so happens I do and my business here is done. Let's blouse."

She followed him toward a sleek white car.

"Zounds, is this yours?" Penelope asked in surprise.

"It is for tonight, doll," he said, opening the door for her.

Penelope once again decided not to ask any further questions.

After letting her in, Tommy got in on his side and started the car up. They took off with a jolt and he entered traffic without bothering to look both ways. A chorus of honking horns serenaded them as he sped away. The piles of snow from the major winter storm that had heralded in the new year had either been cleared or melted so the streets were navigable once again. He somehow wound his way through the clog of other cars at full speed, even going into oncoming traffic if he wanted to pass. Lucky for him, the policemen that used to guide traffic at intersections had been replaced with traffic lights over the past several years, not that Tommy paid any attention to them.

"Where to, Pen?"

"35th, off of Lexington."

He gave her an irritated glance and she shrugged apologetically. Yes, it was a bit of a drive from 137th street, and for good reason. Her reputation among her own set, or at least what used to be her set, was bad enough as it was. Of course, most of them lived closer to Central Park on 5th or Park Avenue. Still, she couldn't very well get caught gambling anywhere near her current neighborhood, not that there were many such establishments located there, at least none that she knew of. Poor Cousin Cordelia would have fainted dead.

"So, what trouble did you get into tonight?"

"Oh, the usual," Penelope replied leaving it perfectly ambiguous. No need to give Tommy too much information about her business.

But he wasn't dumb, and by now he was well acquainted with her reputation with cards. He laughed. "How much did you take him for?"

"Wouldn't you like to know." This earned her an even heartier laugh but no further inquiries, thank goodness.

Now that she was safely out of harm's way and Tommy wasn't pressing the issue, she felt herself relaxing to enjoy the ride as he turned east on North Central Park. This was certainly more thrilling, not to mention faster than the long subway ride that had brought her up to Harlem. Riding in a car was such fun and she so rarely got to do it, even as common as cars were these days. When she was a little girl the street would have still been mostly populated with horses pulling carriages or carts. As terrifying as Tommy's driving was, she much preferred this mode of transportation.

Tommy turned onto her relatively quiet street, not bothering to slow down or pay much attention to other drivers. The sounds of honking horns announced their displeasure.

"Oh Tommy, you devil, you'll wake the neighborhood! More importantly, my cousin."

He just laughed in response, not caring at all.

"I'm right up here," she said pointing to the building where she lived with Cousin Cordelia in a quaint two-bedroom apartment on the second floor.

He parked, then turned to her with a devilish grin. "Say Pen, when are you gonna introduce me to this cousin of yours?"

She laughed, imagining that absurd scenario. "You'd be the death of her, Tommy."

"Ladykiller. I like it."

"I'll bet you do," she said, hoping he wasn't being literal.

"Better question, when are you gonna quit all this nonsense playin' cards and come work for Mr. Sweeney?"

"That would be the death of *me*," she scoffed.

"He could always use a smart dame like you."

"I'm in enough trouble as it is, Tommy. No need to go looking for more."

"Like you did tonight?"

"What do you know about tonight?" Pen asked, feeling sudden pinpricks along her spine.

"You didn't happen to play cards with a man by the name of Rademacher did you? Pinstripe suit fitting little snug in the waist, pencil mustache, too confident for his own good?"

Rademacher. So that was his last name. She gave Tommy a wary look. "What if I did?"

Tommy leaned in and the smile he sported gave a new meaning to the term devilish. "Then I'd say your nights of playing cards might just be coming to an end. Too bad for you he knows some very important people and likes to hold grudges. Mr. Rademacher don't like to lose, especially to a dame. "

"Oh he doesn't does he? And who is *he* to say if I play or not?" she protested.

It was a stupid question. In her old life among the Astors and Vanderbilts who you knew was everything. Upsetting the wrong member of society could be ruinous— as she could personally attest to.

It was no different in the world of the Morellos and Sweeneys. Mr. Rademacher was apparently more influential than she had assumed when she sat down to play with him.

Tommy didn't directly answer the question for her when he responded. "Mr. Sweeney could make it so you never have to worry about who you play cards with again. He knows how much you enjoy it."

"There's a bit more to it than simple enjoyment. It happens to be a significant source of income for me," she said, her words clipped with irritation.

"He could help you out there as well," he crooned.

Once upon a time that deep, melodious timbre of his seemed attractive in a dangerously thrilling sort of way. Now it just felt slimy.

An idea suddenly occurred to her. "Was tonight a setup?"

"Nothing in this world is left to fate, Pen, you know that."

Why, oh why hadn't she listened to Lulu! Pen had just assumed she was being overly cautious. In retrospect that was a rarity for Lucille, which should have told Penelope something; she knew Pen wasn't some naïve duckling anymore. She had known this would be the game to do Pen in and tried to warn her off playing, even if it meant upsetting Mr. Sweeney's obvious trap.

"So just because some...*man*," she uttered the word with contempt, "can't handle losing at cards to a woman, *I'm* the one who has to be punished? Frankly, a man who probably wouldn't otherwise give two figs about losing a hundred dollars, at least based on the looks of him."

Tommy remained perfectly impassive during her tirade, amused even. "It was bound to happen sooner or later, Pen. There are already rumors around town about you maybe being a cheat."

Her mouth fell open in shock. "I've never once cheated!"

Tommy simply shrugged. "I wouldn't blame you if you had, especially since you do it in a way that makes it so's you don't get caught. Why do you think Mr. Sweeney is so interested in you?"

"You tell Mr. Sweeney, thanks but no thanks," Penelope snapped, opening her car door. She wondered if Tommy fortuitously being there to give her a ride home when she needed it was also something that wasn't left to fate.

"You know where to find me if you change your mind, Miss Penelope Banks," he said in a way that was almost formal in its courteousness.

"Thank you for the rescue, *Sir Callahan*," she retorted,

her voice oozing contempt as she slammed the car door shut.

"Anytime, Lady Pen." Tommy laughed as he started the car up. He sped off with a screech of tires that left her wincing. With any luck, Cousin Cordelia would still be fast asleep, none the wiser of Pen's nighttime activities.

Though it seemed those activities were now at an end.

Penelope stormed up the steps, only slowing down once she was out of the cold and inside the front entrance. She fell back against the door to absorb this new reality. She hadn't been lying about cards being a significant source of income for her. Frankly, it's what helped keep Cousin Cordelia and her living a comfortable existence, including the rent on this apartment.

But as Tommy had said, Penelope was a smart "dame." Certainly she could put this brain of hers to good use to earn more money somehow. Frankly, she didn't have much choice.

CHAPTER TWO

"GOOD MORNING, COUSIN CORDELIA," PENELOPE announced late Saturday morning as she took the seat at the breakfast table. Despite last night's upsetting news, a smile came to her face as she imagined Tommy meeting the woman sitting across from her only to realize her dear cousin was probably older than his mother.

"Good morning, Penelope," Cousin Cordelia greeted in a pleasant enough voice.

Penelope wasn't fooled. There wasn't a morning that went by where her cousin didn't fill her ear with the latest evil terrorizing her nerves.

Cousin Cordelia was the first cousin of Penelope's father. She was now a widow and had willingly taken Penelope in after her father had so mercilessly cut her off. When Pen's father, in retaliation, had also decided to end the monthly allowance he'd been giving Cousin Cordelia, she had vehemently dismissed the idea of Penelope leaving. For that, she would forever hold a place in Pen's heart.

Besides, Penelope rather liked living here, mostly for the amusement and companionship it provided. She sensed the feeling was mutual. Cousin Cordelia always remarked how refreshing it was to have a "bright young thing" around—she had always been an anglophile and Penelope didn't have the heart to tell her that term only applied to Londoners—even if she herself lived as though she would have preferred the world coming to a stop at the turn of the century.

"Did you sleep well?" Penelope asked.

"Yes, dear," her cousin replied in an idle tone.

Pen suffered a moment of astonishment at the rare morning where she wouldn't be entertained by her cousin's tales of woe.

Cousin Cordelia was a stubborn sort, set in her ways with a strenuous objection to anything that fell under the heading of "change." She had remained faithful to her shirt-waists and long skirts. Her hair was still unfashionably long and piled atop her head in puffs that had lost favor over a decade ago.

"Well, I suppose a restful night's sleep is a nice change from the usual," Penelope remarked.

Cousin Cordelia's gaze suddenly became more alert, those bright blue eyes they had both inherited from the Banks side of the family igniting with outrage. "Though I did hear the most upsetting noise at a rather obscene hour of the night! Or should I say morning, considering the time."

"Oh?" Penelope asked with innocently wide eyes.

"A *motor car*, speeding down the street as though we lived on some raceway. Horns honking. Tires squealing. All while decent people are trying to sleep. It's a sign of the times, dear Penelope," she moaned, her face a perfect portrait of despair. "And to think this was once a decent neighborhood. Soon there will be pool halls and betting parlors situated right beneath us. Oh, what would dear

Harold think, me practically living in a den of iniquity!"
She fell back in her chair, hand pressed to chest.

Penelope nibbled her toast and waited.

"*Sarah*, my medicine!"

A smile came to Penelope's mouth, which Cousin
Cordelia deliberately ignored.

Sarah, the housemaid who tended to them during the
day skittered in like a scared mouse carrying a glass flask of
amber liquid. Although Cousin Cordelia was a lamb, she
wasn't the easiest woman to tend to; the matron of the
household was particularly needy.

"Just a splash, dear. It is morning after all," Cousin
Cordelia cautioned, still collapsed in her chair as she
awaited the recuperative effects of her "medicine."

Said medicine was actually bootleg brandy. Once upon
a time, Cousin Cordelia did in fact have a legal prescription
for it—just one of the many loopholes to that pesky Prohibition. Her doctor had prescribed it for a temporary malaise
she had suffered over one thing or another. The humiliation
of actually filling it had been more than she could stomach.
Fortunately, Penelope was able to step in and suggest the
services of another "pharmacy" that could satisfy all her
cousin's refills without comment, fuss, or judgement...or a
current prescription. Yet another area where Lulu had been
invaluable.

Sarah obediently tipped the flask just enough for a
splash to land in the small glass, per Cousin Cordelia's
instruction.

"I said a splash," Cousin Cordelia protested with a
frown and one eyebrow raised in reproach.

Sarah began to fret until Penelope winked and smiled at
her, then gestured with her finger and thumb as to how

much "a splash" should be, at least according to her cousin's generous standard of measurement.

"Oh," Sarah acknowledged with mild shock. Penelope had a feeling this would be another maid who wouldn't last very long. True, ladies of decent society shouldn't indulge so wantonly in these times of enforced teetotaling but every woman had her needs. Some people could be so judgmental about these things!

"Gracious me, is that all there is?" Cordelia asked in horror when she saw how little was left in her flask. She took it from Sarah and lifted it to inspect the meager amount that remained of the contents.

"I'm afraid so, ma'am," Sarah said, her cheeks coloring.

"Hrumph," Cordelia grumbled, giving her new maid a look of suspicion.

This sometimes happened. Cousin Cordelia was wont to sip a tad more than she thought she had and was always surprised at how quickly her medicine ran out.

Penelope, of course, could have told her every single instance she had taken a "dose," and just how much had been left in the bottle subsequent to that. It did look a tad lower than she remembered, which meant her cousin had been nipping a bit more than usual after the breakfast hour. Cousin Cordelia's nerves must have been especially taxed lately.

"I'll go out and pick up a new bottle today," Penelope said.

"You will, dear?" Cousin Cordelia replied, brightening up as she held the near-empty bottle out toward Sarah. "Oh, bless you, Penelope. I don't know what I'd do without my prescription from Dr. Peterson."

The fact that Cousin Cordelia's doctor-prescribed refills

had expired almost two years ago was something they both conveniently ignored.

Offering to buy more was an absurd gesture considering their new circumstances, which Penelope was loath to tell her about until she absolutely had to. Still, she couldn't very well deny Cousin Cordelia her one and only personal indulgence. She was otherwise quite happy to live a simple, affordable existence. This was part of the reason they were both able to survive on such a limited amount.

Cousin Cordelia's dearly departed husband Harold Davies may have been the love of her life and a man about which she wouldn't hear a bad word said, but he had bungled management of the healthy sum he'd been left by his father. Cousin Cordelia had been left with only a small savings to carry her through after her husband had passed. It was barely enough to afford this apartment, which was why the allowance from Pen's father had been so helpful, at least until it was unceremoniously cut off.

Thus, when Penelope had started earning an "astounding amount" from her job as a bookkeeper, they had both breathed a bit easier. Cousin Cordelia had no idea that the vast majority of that money came from illegal gambling, and as far as Pen was concerned, she never would. Now, she just had to think of a way to replace that money, and quickly.

She could take the train up to Atlantic City and gamble there, where it was legal. Just the thought of making that trip left Penelope exhausted.

"You're looking tired, dear. I assume your sleep was troubled just as mine was?"

"Hmm?" Penelope hummed, eyebrows raised over her cup of coffee. "Oh no, my night was...uneventful. I feel fine."

"It must be your youth. Oh, how I wish I could sleep through the night as you do. Even a wee dose of my medicine rarely works these days," she said with a resigned sigh, her complaints exhausted for the morning.

Meanwhile, Penelope continued to ponder her options. She considered asking Mr. Brown for a raise. She had been working for him for almost three years now with no increase in income, and had essentially been doing his job for him. Surely another five dollars a week wouldn't be too much to ask. Except, even a five-dollar-a-week raise wouldn't make up for the much larger amount she earned at night playing cards.

There was of course another option.

Not everyone from Pen's old life had abandoned her. There was one person she could have easily relied on, her late mother's dear older friend, Agnes Sterling. Agnes had been like a sister to Penelope's late mother, even though she was over ten years her senior. For some reason she had found Penelope just as fascinating, always indulging her interest in puzzles and memory games.

Pen hadn't turned to Agnes to beg for money even three years ago when, at first, it had all seemed so hopeless. Today, she once again dismissed the thought.

It wasn't just a matter of pride that kept Penelope from reaching out to Agnes. It was that, while almost everyone from her old life considered her a pariah, Agnes was one of the few people who treated her as though nothing had changed. In fact, she seemed rather proud of the fact that Penelope had found her own way in life. Pen was certain the illicit nature of it impressed Agnes even more. She had never been one to abide by the rules of society.

At the very least, Penelope would exhaust all her

options before turning to Agnes, hat in hand. First and foremost, she'd ask Mr. Brown for a raise come Monday.

After breakfast, Penelope left to run errands, specifically to get Cousin Cordelia's medicinal brandy. Now that she was soon to be skint, the ten dollars she spent on Cousin Cordelia's brandy—highway robbery!—was all the more dear.

"I have your medicine," Penelope announced as she entered the apartment. Her cousin was in the sitting room awaiting her arrival.

"Oh, last time it was in such a pretty wrapping, complete with a bow; it looked just like a present," Cousin Cordelia commented, a look of disappointment on her face as she accepted the brown paper package tied with a string.

The packaging, pretty wrapping paper or not, served a purpose. The police were hardly likely to go to the trouble of asking a woman to unwrap a present or package she might be carrying. Penelope had seen illegal liquor housed in all manner of clever camouflage, everything from hollowed-out secret compartments in books or canes to right out in the open in bottles of Coca-Cola, perfume, or medicine vials.

"Bless you, Penelope. Though...I fear you may need a dose yourself. I have news," Cousin Cordelia said, then paused for effect before continuing. She loved drama, so long as it didn't personally affect her or her nerves. Penelope waited patiently. "Your father has invited you to dinner tonight. Promptly at eight o'clock."

"My father? Tonight?" That certainly was news.

"What do you suppose he wants?" Cousin Cordelia observed her with a piercing look, as though Penelope had deliberately been keeping something from her.

"I have no idea." Penelope was just as perplexed as her

cousin. She certainly wasn't on speaking terms with her father, which Cousin Cordelia knew perfectly well. His one allowance was a yuletide dinner, an invitation that even her cousin had always insisted that Penelope accept out of Christian duty. Usually, that meant blessedly never seeing him again until the next Christmas.

Cousin Cordelia sniffed with indignation. "I suppose I shouldn't be surprised that he didn't extend an invitation to me as well."

"Applesauce," Penelope countered, trying to cheer her up. "Do you really want to spend the evening with him for company? I have indigestion just thinking about it."

Cousin Cordelia still looked put out even though she wasn't particularly fond of him either.

"I promise to tell you all the gossip I learn from him," Penelope teased.

Cordelia pursed her lips then laughed. They both know Pen's father was the last person to gossip about anything, at least anything interesting. Yet another mark against him in the eyes of Cordelia.

Pen considered the idea that she could decline the invitation, being that her father no longer had a say in her life. But she was curious. After three years of almost no communication other than the obligatory sort, he suddenly wanted an audience.

How could she refuse?

CHAPTER THREE

Since Penelope's father hadn't seen fit to send a car for her, and she couldn't very well afford to splurge on a taxi, she took the Eastside subway line up to 59th Street and walked from there.

She needn't have worried about being on her own in this part of town, even after dark. No one was likely to commit any felonies this close to the Vanderbilts' magnificent mansion that sat across from the southeast corner of Central Park. Pen stopped to admire the French chateau style. She was probably one of the few people walking along the street right now who had been inside as a guest.

While Penelope did sometimes miss the uncomplicated ease and luxury of that existence, her life had certainly been more exciting since being shunned by the privileged classes. She'd probably learned more in the past three years than she had in the twenty-one years prior to that, at least with regard to anything of practical use. And she'd had a lot more fun doing it.

She continued up 5th Avenue along the park, passing other mansions and the luxury apartments that were creeping in to replace them. The Banks had lived in a mansion just past 62nd street since before Penelope was born.

Coleman, the Banks' longtime butler met her at the door with the same professional demeanor he might have shown King George himself, even though he'd known her since she was a precocious little girl.

"Good evening Coleman, how are you?" she greeted warmly, a genuine smile on her face.

"Very fine, thank you, Miss Penelope," he returned, which was about as familiar as he ever was with her. It was the one indication, beneath his stiff-shirt facade, that he felt the same affection toward her that she did toward him. "Your father is in the dining room. Please follow me."

After handing over her coat and gloves, she trailed him past the threshold and instantly felt herself transported back in time. The white marble floor of the foyer was the same she had run across as a child, earning the indulgent tutting of her mother, and eventual roars for silence from her father, which had only ever caused Penelope to giggle with impish delight.

She paused to look up at the full-length portrait done of her mother when she had first married Penelope's father. The large, crystal chandelier cast a glittering light that gave it an even more awe-inducing glow.

Juliette Williams had only been nineteen when she became Juliette Banks, marrying a man fifteen years her senior. The pink ruffles and silk roses decorating her waist and the demure neckline belied the mischievous hint that colored her soft smile and green eyes. It was as though she knew it was all a facade. It had probably been some concession to her new husband, a presentation of demure femininity to mask the daring woman underneath. Perhaps even

Reginald Banks had known at the time and enjoyed the mild bit of subterfuge presented to the public.

No, Penelope could never see fit to be that generous in her thoughts about her father.

If only her mother hadn't become one of the many victims of the Great Influenza in 1919. Before that, she'd been the main source of joy and vibrancy in this mansion, which now felt decidedly like a mausoleum.

Coleman politely coughed to catch her attention.

"Yes, yes," Penelope sang, forcing her attention away from the painting. "Dinner awaits!"

Her father was already seated in the dining room. He cast a hard look upon Penelope as she entered, no doubt searching for any recent flaws that would confirm his continuing disappointment in her.

"Dear *papah*, it's been far too long."

Papa was unamused. He gestured to the seat next to him where he sat at the head of the table that could usually accommodate twelve.

Before her mother died that table would have been filled with a mix of interesting guests: opera singers conversing with philosophers; writers arguing with politicians; artists pontificating with scientists. With her mother, it could be any or all of the above.

A rare fight had once erupted between her parents when her mother had invited Scott Joplin, the "King of Ragtime" to dine with their guests. "Foreigners" and "libertines" were one thing, a colored man was beyond the pale (so to speak) for Reginald Banks. But only Mama could soften her father enough to have him cater to her every wish, even one that left decent society positively scandalized—and then had them clamoring for a seat at one of her next infamous dinners.

"To what do I owe the pleasure of an invitation?" she asked, her curiosity getting the better of her.

"Not before the soup course," her father scolded.

She knew he preferred a captive audience when discussing important matters. So this wasn't a social call after all, not that she'd been under any illusion it was.

Penelope sighed and sat under his scrutinizing gaze, which lingered unfavorably on her dress. She was wearing a gold Jean Patou, but he wouldn't have known that. It was the first high-end "modern" dress—all draped silk, bare arms, and beaded bodice—she had bought after her first big win at cards. That was back when she assumed the kale would be free-flowing. If only she'd known just how precarious Cousin Cordelia's financial situation, and thus hers, had been at the time. Silly girl.

"Are you wearing rouge on your lips?" he asked, peering closer with a decidedly disapproving look.

"Not before the soup course," she replied with mock reproof.

His lips tightened with anger. In response, hers—yes, colored with rouge, or rather lipstick—did as well, if only to hold back a laugh.

Why did she love irking him so?

"Something to drink, Miss Penelope?" Coleman offered.

"Champagne?" Penelope inquired with a daring grin.

"Impudence is unbecoming," her father admonished.

"Such a shame a woman can no longer have a glass of wine with her meal."

"What would you know about wine or champagne?"

"I'm twenty-four not fourteen, Papa. Prohibition began only five years ago. I *do* remember the good old days."

Her father made a sound that expressed his thoughts on "the good old days."

"Prohibition was a necessary evil to curb an even worse evil. From what I can see it has been an overall positive for society."

"I think you and I have vastly different vantage points from which to view society," she replied with an arched brow, before requesting a ginger ale.

He narrowed his eyes to study her. "What have you been getting yourself involved with?"

"Oh you know, voting, dancing the Charleston at integrated nightclubs, drinking in speakeasies—"

"And you wonder why I'd have seen you married!" he practically roared, not bothering to hide his exasperation. "This is exactly the sort of trouble an unmarried, *modern* woman gets herself into. You should have wedded Clifford Stokes and none of this would be an issue."

"No, the only issue would be him *canoodling* with Patience Gilmore, which is exactly what I caught him doing the night before our wedding was to take place!"

"There's no need for such vulgar language. As for that nonsense, that's no excuse to simply fail to show up at the altar, Penelope. The invitations had already been sent out, for heaven's sake. There hadn't even been enough time to inform the guests! There are less problematic ways of handling these sorts of things. You wouldn't be the first woman to look the other way while her husband—"

"Did Mama look the other way?" Penelope interrupted in shock.

"Of course not, she had no reason to!" Thankfully, father had the decency to look highly offended.

Penelope relaxed with relief. She may not have particularly liked her father, but she would have hated him if he'd had affairs while married to her mother.

"The point is, there are more important things than what a man gets up to in private, so long as he's discreet about it."

"And here I thought marriage implied fidelity. How foolish of me."

"If you two hadn't had such a brief courtship, recklessly getting engaged after only knowing the fellow for a few months, you might have learned this about him before agreeing to be his wife. What with that strange affliction you've been cursed with, one would have thought it would finally do you some good."

Penelope didn't bother telling him that wasn't exactly how her "strange affliction" worked. Just because she could recall things with perfect clarity didn't mean she couldn't still be blind to what was right in front of her. But that was neither here nor there, and Penelope just wished she could forget about the whole thing.

Coleman came back with her ginger ale. It was in a champagne coupe which she thought was a rascally touch. So he wasn't completely lacking in a sense of humor after all.

Her father droned on. "There were other factors to consider at the time, Penelope. Such as the important business relationships I am still mending to this day. Clifford Stokes comes from an influential family worth millions. To have embarrassed them in the manner that you did was disastrous. Is it any wonder you are no longer invited to the parties and social events of your peers? They at least understand propriety and decorum."

Penelope felt the sting of that reminder. She knew her old friends couldn't have given two figs about propriety and decorum. All they cared about was status and money, and she currently had neither.

Father gave her a satisfied smile, as though reading her mind. "It isn't too late, Penelope. Even though you are older and perhaps too liberal in your ways, we can iron all of that out and make you a proper wife to a suitable husband."

"I think I'd prefer my job as a bookkeeper," she replied dryly, yet truthfully.

Father shook his head with dismay, no doubt wondering how he had become so cursed in life.

When the mushroom soup arrived, Penelope demurely took a leisurely sip, then set her spoon down. "Now then, to what do I owe the pleasure?"

"Agnes Sterling," he replied in a tone that perfectly expressed his unfavorable feelings about the woman. Agnes had, of course, been a frequent guest at Mama's dinners.

"Agnes? That fun old gal?" Penelope exclaimed, brightening up. The term of endearment was Agnes's own description of herself, and always gave Penelope a good laugh. "What about her?"

"You've been summoned to her home in Long Island. You're to arrive before Monday morning."

"Monday? In January? Whatever for?" Long Island was enjoyable in the summer when society escaped the heat of the city, and a party was held every other night. In the winter it was dreary and isolated.

"That 'fun old gal' has passed away," he said solemnly.

Penelope gasped, her spoon splashing into her soup as her grip loosened from shock. She sagged in her chair as the rest of her body went slack. "She's dead? What happened?"

"Suicide." She could hear the judgement in his voice. "It apparently happened last night. They found her this morning."

"Suicide?" she repeated, sitting up straighter with indignation. "I refuse to believe it!"

"That is what the police are claiming. I'm far more inclined to have confidence in their assessment over your *beliefs*. It does make some bit of sense. I wasn't overly fond of the woman but I would have never wished her fate on anyone."

"Applesauce," Penelope retorted.

The car accident Agnes had suffered in late summer, forcing her into a wheelchair, had done nothing to dampen her spirit. The last time Penelope had seen her was at her New Year's Eve party here in the city. Even then she had been discussing her plans for her notorious summer parties at her home in Long Island. That was not the act of a woman intent on killing herself.

Penelope stared at her father, still absorbing the news. In retrospect, she should have realized something was wrong when news about Agnes had come from him of all people. Agnes would have never used him as a messenger for anything. Just the fact that he could be so cold and callous as he delivered the news....

But he'd been like that after Mama's death as well, turning to stone and maintaining a stiff upper lip, even in the confines of their home away from public view.

Penelope, on the other hand, was now a bubbling cauldron of emotion, not the least of which was guilt. She'd had no idea that her old friend was already dead this morning when she'd briefly flirted with the idea of asking Agnes for money. Now the thought left a sick feeling in the pit of her stomach.

"So you invite me to dinner all so you can gloat as you tell me such terrible news?"

She was surprised to see a flash of shock and hurt touch

his gaze. "I'm hardly gloating, Penelope. I know you and I were...never as close as you were to your mother, but I would never be that callous. The fact is, her attorney Mr. Wilcox and I are acquainted with one another. He thought it best if the news came from me."

"He was no doubt familiar with your warm and comforting nature," she retorted.

Father ignored that, any hint of emotion he had momentarily suffered now disappearing. "No, but he is familiar with the fact that I am well-versed in business and, to a certain extent, the law. Which is why I'm the one imparting the additional news that she has named you as a beneficiary in her will."

"What? Me?"

"Yes. It's to be read at ten a.m. Monday morning."

"She's probably taken pity on my circumstances and left me a tidy sum to get by." She gave her father a pointed, accusatory look.

"Bully for you," he said in a dry tone. "With any hope you'll be sensible about any windfall. I am of course an advocate of stocks, but be cautious. Don't be fooled by the average man making a mint these days. Just because it's been nonstop growth doesn't mean the rise will continue. You're too young to remember the last panic. We're overdue for another. Land and treasuries, in that order. Tried and true investments, both of them."

"Thank you father," Penelope replied, not bothering to hide her contempt. Of course his focus would only be on money. "Though Agnes seemed to do alright buying art these days. Several modern pieces of hers are already worth quite a large sum, not that she would ever sell."

Would have ever sold, she had to remind herself, feeling the sorrow overcome her again.

"Modern art," father scoffed. "A bunch of lines and shapes thrown together in some semblance of an object or person. Any child could do the same. I thought Van Gogh and then that Klimt fellow were bad enough in my day. Bring back the Renaissance I say, a period when a man knew how to paint." He raised one censuring brow. "And a woman knew how to marry."

"Who knows? Perhaps she's left me a suitable husband."

"With any luck, she has."

Penelope honestly believed he wished that, even above the possibility of inheriting the entirety of Agnes's fortune, which was quite substantial.

Suddenly Penelope had no appetite for soup or anything else. Frankly, she could no longer stand to be in the same room as her father, not when she had a dear loved one to grieve.

The sound of her pushing her chair back drew his attention away from his soup. "Where are you going? Dinner has only just begun."

"I'm going home to go drown my sorrows in a bottle of champagne in Agnes's honor." The look on Father's face was almost enough to soothe her pain, if only a little.

Penelope stormed out holding back her tears until she was on the street again. Agnes Sterling was gone. Penelope had no intention of leaving it at suicide. She'd never once seen any hint of self-pity or a desire to end it all in Agnes.

But Pen would focus on that when she traveled to Long Island. For tonight, she was glad she had splurged on the expense of Cousin Cordelia's bottle of "medicine." She planned on taking a very hefty dose.

CHAPTER FOUR

THE NEXT DAY, AFTER MORNING CHURCH SERVICE, Penelope and Cousin Cordelia took the train to Long Island. Mr. Brown had grudgingly given her the day off, though she would have feigned sickness if he hadn't.

Agnes's home was in Glen Cove, where several other millionaires had thought to build their own massive mansions on large swaths of land. The stretches of woody areas shielding each of them from view was a testament to just how much acreage there was to be had out here.

It was a far cry from the slightly claustrophobic compactness and noise of Manhattan, which Penelope had an odd liking for. Still, there was a certain appeal even when the branches were bare and snow clung to the grass.

Leonard, Agnes's chauffeur, was waiting at the station for them when they exited, bundled up against the cold weather. He took their bags and led them to a very nice car, one of several owned by Agnes.

"Oh my," said Cousin Cordelia, frozen in place as the back passenger door was opened for her.

Penelope could understand her hesitation. Beyond her

cousin's entrenched objection to motor cars, she knew that Agnes had suffered her tragic accident while driving one. Despite having a chauffeur, Agnes loved to drive, especially on the often empty roads of Long Island.

"It's perfectly safe, Cousin," Penelope reassured her, getting in first. "After all, Leonard has made it here with no harm. Tell her, Leonard," she insisted.

Leonard, in his early thirties, offered the sort of grin that could win over many a woman. It worked well enough to erode Cousin Cordelia's concerns. "The car is perfectly safe, ma'am. I checked it myself this very morning."

That calmed her cousin's nerves just enough to get her to enter. When it started up, she clung to Penelope's arm, before letting go with an embarrassed laugh.

"I do miss the days of horses," Cousin Cordelia sighed. "A much more dignified means of travel."

Penelope's memory of that time consisted mostly of rather pungent odors and the necessity of watching where one placed one's foot while crossing the street.

"Cars have been around for a while now, Cousin, and there will only be more in the future. You should start getting used to it."

Cousin Cordelia's expression left no question as to what she thought of that.

Penelope smiled and patted her hand reassuringly, then turned to look out the window. The painful effects of last night's overindulgence in "medicine" were finally beginning to wear off. With a clearer head she could focus on how to discover what truly happened to Agnes. Unfortunately, she had left her father's before getting the details.

She thought back to Agnes's party to herald in the new year. Most people had surely attended out of morbid curiosity. Agnes had handled it with perfect aplomb, making jokes at her own expense about having to face the "horrid burden" of being carried about by young, handsome men from now on. She forbade an ounce of pity to darken her disposition.

Penelope choked back a sob with a laugh.

"Are you alright, my dear?" Cousin Cordelia said, patting her arm in sympathy.

"I still don't believe she would kill herself. At the very least, it must have been an accident or some other misadventure. I fully plan on finding out for myself," she added feeling her resolve set in.

"Oh, Penelope, you aren't going to get yourself into trouble, are you? You always did have such a meddlesome nature as a young girl."

Penelope offered a wicked grin. "I suppose it's a good thing I have you with me to act as chaperone."

Cousin Cordelia pursed her lips. "When has anyone ever been able to rein you in? All I ask is that whatever you get up to, don't involve me. I'll have no detailed description of suicide or death in my presence, thank you. I already feel faint thinking about it." She sat up straighter in alarm. "Oh, I've forgotten to bring my medicine!"

Penelope laughed. "One thing I'm certain of is that Agnes had plenty of her own 'medicine' on hand."

Her cousin frowned with disapproval. Illegal alcohol for pure enjoyment was certainly not the same thing as medicinal usage, even if they no doubt came from the same distillery.

They drove through the iron gates of Agnes's estate. Ahead, Penelope could see the water of Long Island Sound through the large windows on the first floor of the mansion. Her eyes slid to the addition Agnes had built after her accident. That addition, which housed her personal suite, was why Agnes spent most of her time in Glen Cove rather than her apartment in Manhattan. The hustle and bustle of people in the crowded city wasn't very accommodating for someone in a wheelchair.

"My, it is rather large isn't it?" Cousin Cordelia observed in awe.

"She did have a lot of money," Penelope pointed out.

Leonard parked in the circular drive and got out to open the car door for Penelope and her cousin. The front door was opened by Chives, Agnes's butler of almost twenty years. She often wondered if that was his real name, but had never dared to ask.

"Miss Banks, Mrs. Davies, welcome," he greeted, lowering his head slightly as he opened the door wider for them to enter. The large foyer was just as grandiose as the outside of the house. It had served as a wondrous welcome to partygoers who were led past the double winding staircase to the French doors that opened to the long terrace and steps leading down to the water.

Cousin Cordelia hummed and fussed over the extravagance of it all as they were escorted upstairs to their rooms. Penelope had called ahead to let them know she would have a guest accompanying her. In this home, it wouldn't have mattered. There were twenty bedrooms, and several cottages dotting the property.

"A late lunch will be served at two o'clock in the dining room. I will have Edith, your maid, sent up to help you get settled. Please let her know if you would like some light refreshment before then. Will there be anything else, Miss Banks? Mrs. Davies?" Chives asked after guiding them in their rooms.

Penelope desperately wanted to ask about Agnes's supposed suicide. As the head of the staff and her most trusted employee, Chives would certainly be informed on the details. However, even Pen with a "meddlesome" nature had better manners than that.

"No thank you, Chives."

He left them to their bedrooms. Penelope closed the door to hers and turned to look out of the large window. It offered a stunning, unobstructed view of the grounds at the rear of the house and the water beyond. Across the sound she could see where New York met Connecticut.

A knock on the door announced Edith's arrival and she turned to greet her maid with a smile. She appeared to be a new hire; Penelope certainly didn't recognize her. She was young, probably a few years younger than Penelope. Her hair was in a dark, chic bob, not too different from her own. She had brown eyes that had a spark of intelligence in them. The rest of her face was pretty in a rather angular fashion, with sharp, clever features.

If she was as smart as she looked, that might explain what had landed her such an enviable position. A grand house in Long Island during the winter months where guests would be infrequent was a rather undemanding situation. Though, perhaps she had only been hired on as a temporary solution for the upcoming influx of guests. Penelope wondered how many others there were and if any of them had arrived yet.

Maids were notorious fountains of information, being so intimately familiar with the needs and wants of guests of the house. She didn't want to get the poor girl in hot water when she'd only just started working here. On the other hand, it wouldn't hurt to ask a few fairly harmless questions.

"Will there be anything else, Miss Banks?" Edith asked, after putting Penelope's things away.

"You're a new hire, aren't you?"

"I am," she replied, giving Penelope a wary look.

"I only ask out of sympathy," Penelope quickly explained. "I can't imagine starting a position only to have your employer...pass away. When did you start?"

"Only just this past Monday, ma'am."

That recently? It was certainly a surprise. Still, she'd started before Agnes's death, which was helpful.

"Suicide, such a tragedy. Was it an overdose of medication?" Penelope drew upon what she assumed was the most likely cause of death in the case of suicide.

"I was told it was poison," Edith responded, her brow wrinkled in confusion.

"Poison?" Penelope supposed that was another common method, though certainly not a pleasant nor dignified one. It only made her more suspicious.

She figured it would be "meddlesome" to ask if Edith had seen any indication that Agnes wanted to commit suicide.

"I'm sorry, I shouldn't press you for such personal infor-mation. I'm sure the police have already asked you similar questions."

"Not really ma'am. The only people they talked to were Chives, and Beth."

Beth was Agnes's long time personal maid. She was as trusted an employee as Chives was. Penelope would be very curious to talk with her. Had she heard anything? A cry of pain or sounds of a disturbance? What had Agnes been like that night?

The police had no doubt asked the same questions to be so sure in their assessment of suicide.

"Only Chives and Beth?"

"Well, of the staff. They also questioned the other guests."

"Other guests? Agnes had company that night?" This wasn't entirely surprising. Agnes was not only popular but generous with her accommodations. She would have never objected to having guests over for dinner and then offering them a room for the night. Though, this time of year there couldn't have been many neighbors or guests.

"Who were the guests that night?"

"There was a Major Hallaway and his, er, wife." Penelope caught the small, sardonic twitch in Edith's lips at the mention of his wife. "There was also Mrs. Mayweather."

So far none of the names struck a note of familiarity for Penelope.

"Are any of the guests still here?" She wouldn't mind doing a bit of subtle interrogation if they were, even if the police had already done so.

"Oh yes ma'am, all of them are staying through tomorrow I've been told."

"Really?" Penelope was almost daft enough to ask if they were the other beneficiaries named in Agnes's will. Of course there would be no way for Edith of all people to know that. But why else would they stay on? "Are there any other guests arriving for tomorrow?"

"A Mr. Raymond Colley I believe. I've been told he's a regular visitor though; has his own room and everything. But he wasn't here that night."

That *was* a name familiar to Penelope. He was Agnes's nephew, taken in by her two years ago after some hullabaloo in St. Louis with his father. His mother, Agnes's sister, had died when Raymond was a baby. Agnes had never taken a liking to her sister's husband, who had apparently been as much of a tyrant with his son as he had been with his wife.

From what Penelope had seen of Raymond the son had fallen as far from that tree as possible.

Raymond had been set up at some investment house in the financial district, selling bonds like many idle young men from wealthy families. That didn't mean he was anything resembling a stiff shirt. Only a few years younger than Pen, he'd been a frequent attendee at Agnes's parties, and was rather popular with the young ladies.

"Will that be all ma'am?" Edith asked, studying Penelope with anxious eyes.

"Yes, thank you, Edith."

Edith gave a small curtsy before leaving, which made Penelope smile. She really must be new. Even the stuffier households didn't require such fawning gestures.

After she left, Penelope sat in the window seat overlooking the water and thought about what she'd learned. Most of the people staying here through Monday had also been here the night of Agnes's death. It was too much of a coincidence for Penelope to ignore.

CHAPTER FIVE

PENELOPE'S FIRST STOP BEFORE LUNCH WAS DOWN TO Agnes's suite. She wanted to see for herself if any tell-tale clues would indicate foul play.

Her suite was located down a short hallway not too far from the staff area. This had been by design. With Agnes's new limitations, it was helpful to have the staff able to arrive at a moment's notice.

Once there, Penelope found the door locked.

Aside from Agnes, she knew both Beth and Chives had keys, but Penelope wondered who else had one, and where they were kept. There were no signs that anyone might have forced the door. Surely that would have had even the most inept police reconsidering suicide.

With no access to the suite, she set out in search of either Beth or Chives. When she didn't find them in the main part of the house, she made her way back toward the staff area.

There was a hallway that led to a small open area where one could get to the individual staff quarters, the kitchen, and the butler's study. As she approached, she could hear Chives's voice as he spoke to the kitchen staff.

Penelope passed through the open area, casting a quick glance up to the recently electrified bell system so guests could page members of the staff. The original bells had been replaced by sound buzzers.

When Pen's mother had brought her here to visit as a child she had delighted in sneaking into these servants' areas and watching the bells swing and give off a tinkling sound, especially when the mansion was abuzz with active guests. On occasion she had even been known to jump up and slap a bell just to see what would happen.

Perhaps Cousin Cordelia did have a point about her being meddlesome. As an adult, one who wouldn't dare do such a thing, the bells were one of the few quaint relics of the past she missed. The modern buzzers, now located well above her reach even if she were inclined to act the brat, made everything seem so business-like and impersonal.

She stopped to consider them. Had the one for Agnes's suite sounded at all that night? Perhaps it had come too late to do anything for her.

Penelope continued on to find Chives speaking with Arabella, the cook, and the two girls who helped in the kitchen, Kelly and Kate. Penelope had always thought that was an amusingly alliterative name pairing, though they looked nothing alike. Kelly was short and quite plump with bright red hair and freckles, while Kate was taller and exceedingly thin with brown hair and dark eyes.

On the counter, Penelope could see the cold chicken, Waldorf salad, and other dishes prepared for the late lunch.

"I'm sorry to interrupt, Chives. Hello, Arabella. Kelly. Kate," she greeted with a smile.

"Oh Miss Banks, isn't it just so terrible!" Arabella cried.

"You poor dear, you must be particularly distraught. Miss Sterling did dote on you so, didn't she? Then again, you have the look of your mother, don't you just? That one was just like Miss Sterling—two peas in a pod, I says! It's no wonder she was always going on about you, talking about how smart you were with those puzzles and such. Of course, Miss Sterling always was generous with the compliments, wasn't she? Never had a bad word to say about anyone, even those who could have used a bad word or two." She raised one censuring eyebrow to stress the point.

Penelope knew Arabella to be as dramatic and long-winded as her name, with a penchant for ending most sentences in a rhetorical question.

"It is terrible, I still can't believe it," Penelope commiserated.

"Suicide, hrumph! That lovely woman would no sooner commit suicide than kick a puppy."

Kate gasped and turned red. Chives silently exhaled and briefly closed his eyes. Kelly was oblivious. Penelope tactfully refrained from reacting, mostly because she knew Arabella hadn't meant the suggestion with any malice. It had been quite some time since Agnes had lost the functioning use of her legs.

Arabella simply continued. "And those police officers coming in here asking questions about my food, but did you see any of the others keeling over? No you did *not*! I even had a little something leftover for Mr. Colley when he came whistling outside my window in the wee hours like we was Romeo and Juliet," she said with a schoolgirl titter.

"Really? What time was that?" Penelope asked, with a laugh just to mask her suspicions.

"Goodness me, I'd say...oh, about one in the morning? Well into his cups, wasn't he though? Never mind he'd been

COLETTE CLARK

driving that car he loves so much. But he and all the others were fine as could be after eating Arabella's cooking, were they not? Though, again if I had my druthers—"

"Thank you, Arabella, please see that lunch is ready promptly by two," Chives tactfully interrupted.

"Oh look at me, our sweet Miss Banks has come to look in on us and see how we're coping and me not even offering a treat. Gingersnaps! I think this time of year is perfect for them, no? They're up in the pantry over there. Kelly, fetch the stool and—"

"Oh, please no. I really shouldn't. After all lunch is about to be served," Penelope pleaded, not wanting to put them out. She had only come to the kitchen seeking Chives.

Kelly had already eagerly picked up the stepping stool, which was located next to the entryway of the open area that led toward the staff's rooms. Despite Penelope's protests, the gingersnap cookies were procured from the higher shelf.

"Mercy me, I thought for sure there was more than this!" Arabella exclaimed in surprise when the tin was opened. Both she and Kate cast accusing looks toward Kelly.

"It wasn't me!" Kelly protested, though her rosy cheeks gave her away. "In fact, I caught that Mrs. Mayweather back here sneaking some for herself late—"

"Kelly!" Chives scolded, casting a harsh look of reproach that had her cowering into silence.

Penelope bit back a smile at the girl's talking out of turn. She wasn't used to guests being back here to overhear.

"All the same, I think we could all use a little sweetness in these trying times, no?" Arabella said, effortlessly moving on. "Mrs. Sterling was a true lady, even with all that carrying on every summer having guests in and out—and

40

those parties! Mercy me," Arabella shook her head with wonder. "Still, she always gave fair warning to yours truly, thank you very much, even when there were only as few as two souls joining her for dinner. Though this week certainly caused us both a bit of a surprise, don't you know? Then again, the poor dear obviously had a lot on her mind, didn't she? I suppose I could forgive her the lack of notice."

Arabella's expression became morose and she closed her eyes. Kelly took advantage of the moment to sneak a few gingersnaps while Kate looked on with disapproval.

"Allow me to escort you back into the drawing room, Miss Banks. Lunch will be starting soon." Penelope followed Chives out.

"So Raymond was in fact here Friday night?" Penelope confirmed.

"Mr. Colley did arrive very late."

So much for Edith being a fountain of information. He had obviously arrived after she'd retired for the night.

Still, leave it to Chives to know everything going on in this house. This of course worked well for Pen's purposes.

She paused, stopping them both now that they were out of hearing range of the staff or any of the other guests. She decided to be perfectly blunt with him. "Do you think it was suicide, Chives?"

He studied her for a moment, no doubt wondering if it would break his professional decorum to answer truthfully, or even at all. "I do not, Miss Banks. I simply can't fathom it."

"Neither can I," she said, glad to have someone else confirm her doubts.

Chives eyes wavered and his brow knitted together in consternation. "It's just that the evidence is—well, I'm not sure what to think of it, Miss Banks."

"Tell me everything."

"Well, there was a final letter unfolded next to her on the bed. Then the bottle of poison? It seemed like it had fallen from her hand. The room was still locked when Beth came in the next morning. None of it makes sense."

That was pretty damning information. A locked room was bad enough, but there was a suicide note and a bottle of poison as well? No wonder the police had declared it a suicide.

"Did you see the letter? Was it in Agnes's handwriting?"

"I read it myself, Miss Banks, after Beth came to collect me. It very much looked like it was written by her hand. And it matched against several other examples of her handwriting."

Penelope felt her hopes sink, but she was determined not to give up.

"Was there anything unusual that night? Anything at all?"

Chives hesitated only a moment.

"What is it?"

"Well, it isn't so much unusual as rare. The...gentleman from whom Miss Sterling procured a regular delivery of various substances."

"Bootleg liquor?" Penelope confirmed with a wry smile.

"Yes, Miss Banks. Barney McClintock. He often sent personal selections for her that were special blends. He liked to keep himself in her good graces, you see. Particularly after how much she had spent for her New Year's party. She enjoyed the clever reuse of containers he had them delivered in—jam jars, milk bottles, one time he even used an hour glass. Friday we had received a sampling from him."

"You said it was rare? How rare?"

"It varied, but once a week was standard. It was rare to receive a delivery twice in one week, but it has happened before. However, Mr. McClintock had already sent a sampling that Monday."

"So, there *was* something unusual that night."

"I myself delivered the package to Miss Sterling after Beth had gotten her settled into bed." His brow wrinkled with worry at what that might indicate.

"Chives, I hope you know I don't suspect you at all," Penelope said, resting a reassuring hand on his arm.

"Of course, Miss Banks." He flashed a brief smile of appreciation.

"This package, did it seem like it had been tampered with?"

"Not at all. It had the usual blue paper he wrapped it in, almost like a gift. This was standard. And why would Mr. McClintock try to poison Miss Sterling?"

Penelope was certain this bottle had held the poison, but Chives had a good point. Barney wouldn't have poisoned her, she was a goose laying golden eggs for him with how much she spent on alcohol.

This meant either it had been delivered with the poison inside, or it had been added after the fact.

"Did Agnes ever once ring for help that night?"

"Not once. Beth is a very light sleeper and never misses a call from Miss Sterling. I also never heard her ring for service. I asked all of the staff and none of them heard it either."

In retrospect, if the poison had been in her nightcap, she may have gone quite quickly. But quickly enough to keep her from exerting the minor effort to reach out and press the call button? That seemed doubtful.

That still didn't explain how the bottle and letter were there with her. Perhaps someone had come in later that night to place them?

"You and Beth both have keys to her suite? Where do you keep them?"

"Both are on the nightstand right next to us for immediate access. Neither of our keys was missing the next morning."

"And Agnes kept her room locked at night?"

"Yes, Miss Banks."

Penelope felt she had exhausted all lines of inquiry for now. It hadn't produced much that she found helpful, at least in terms of negating this as a suicide.

It was time to talk to Beth, who had been the one to see her to bed and, more importantly, find her the next morning.

But there was one final thing she wanted to ask about, something else that had been a change from the usual.

"Edith is new, hired just this week it seems?"

"Do you have any complaints about her service?"

"No, of course not," Penelope quickly assured him. "It's just very interesting timing, don't you think?"

Chives paused and Penelope knew she had touched upon a delicate matter.

"We...had to replace a member of the staff."

"Oh?" she urged, one eyebrow raised in encouragement for him to continue.

"Julia, one of the maids. She was dismissed this past week."

The name propelled an image of the slight young woman, reserved to the point of shyness, to the front of Penelope's mind. In a job that required unobtrusiveness, she had been one to easily blend in with the scenery, barely even squeaking out a word unless directly questioned. Julia had been working here for almost two years now, surely long enough to be considered reliable.

"What in the world could she have possibly done?"

Once again, Chives demurred.

"I'll just find out from another member of the staff," Penelope said with an arched brow and an apologetic smile. This officially fell under the heading "meddlesome."

Chives had the tact not to show any hint of irritation. In fact, there seemed to be a tiny spark of respect in his eyes for her doggedness. "There was a theft."

"A theft? By Julia?" Penelope said in surprise. She tried to picture the mousy little maid having the courage to steal something. It wasn't impossible to imagine—one never knew what lie in people's hearts—but it still came as a bit of a shock.

"A pair of diamond earrings belonging to Mrs. Mayweather, to whom she'd been attending."

"And you know for sure it was Julia who stole them?" Pen knew that staff were often unfairly accused of theft when people had simply mislaid objects or other guests of the house had stolen them.

"The earrings were found in her private effects."

Penelope exhaled. "Well, I suppose that certainly points the finger at her."

"Unequivocally."

"And thus, Edith was hired—rather quickly it seems?"

"She was recommended and did come with references. The Sullivan family as well as the Aldreds."

"I see." Penelope knew the Sullivans and Aldreds from her old life, and a favorable reference from either of those families would certainly be a boon to a maid seeking employment.

Time to move on.

"The guests who were here Friday night, it seems they are also staying through to Monday?" She refrained from being tawdry enough to point out that this meant they were most likely included in the will, but Chives understood the implication.

He paused as though wondering what decorum mandated. "Yes, Mr. Wilcox has specified that all of them should be here on Monday."

So they were all named in the will then. Penelope planned on being just as "meddlesome" with them as she was presently being with Chives, perhaps more so.

"And they all stayed here Friday night?"

"Yes." He was tactful enough not to insinuate anything either in his voice or demeanor.

"When did they arrive?"

"Major and Mrs. Hallaway arrived that Saturday and were originally scheduled to leave yesterday. Mrs. Mayweather is residing at another home in Long Island, Oyster Bay I believe. On evenings when she dines here, Miss Sterling has—*had* taken to offering her a room for the evening."

"How often was that?"

"Quite often. Perhaps a few times a week."

"She should have just moved in, it seems."

Chives was diplomatic enough to remain silent on that matter.

"Are they related to Agnes?"

Agnes had never married or had children herself, which was no doubt why she had lived such an adventurous life. Penelope was still in awe from the tales of Agnes's adventures traveling the world, not to mention the various lovers she'd had.

"Major Hallaway was Miss Sterling's cousin. Mr. Colley is her nephew. As far as I know, Mrs. Mayweather is merely a friend."

"Obviously a *close* friend."

"I wouldn't know Miss Banks."

Chives would be too professional to say anything out of turn as Kelly had. Penelope would have to wait to learn more about these other guests later on at lunch.

"I'd like to speak with Beth. Also, I'd like to have a look at Agnes's suite if I could?"

Chives hesitated before speaking. "I'm afraid I had Miss Sterling's rooms cleaned, Miss Banks. It seemed most fitting, in retrospect, out of respect for Miss Sterling. The state of it that morning was...it seemed inconsiderate to her memory."

Damn!

Penelope refrained from expressing her disappointment. She could hardly fault him for that, especially after the police had confirmed the cause of death. Perhaps there were police photos she could look at instead.

"All the same, perhaps she could walk me through the suite, telling me what happened that night. It might lead to some minor detail that clears this up."

"Of course, Miss Banks. I'll have her sent there right away. Will there be anything else?"

"No, thank you Chives. This has been very helpful."

CHAPTER SIX

Penelope was waiting by Agnes's door when Beth arrived with the key. She had been in service to Agnes since Penelope was a young girl. As Agnes's personal maid, she had even trained with a nurse as to how to best serve Agnes's personal needs once she was in a wheelchair.

The dark circles under Beth's eyes and the numb look on her face were all the indication that Penelope needed to confirm that this had come as a shock to her as well.

"This must have been terrible for you, Beth. I'm so sorry."

She nodded, then a firm set came to her mouth. "If it helps you find out what happened, I'm happy to help, Miss Banks. This has all been so awful."

Penelope smiled sympathetically. "I plan on doing just that."

Beth nodded and unlocked, then opened the door. Penelope followed her in, faltering slightly as the familiar space came into view.

The suite opened into a small entryway. There was a full-length mirror on one side, and on the other side was a small table with two trays. The smaller tray served as a deposit locale for Agnes's key to the suite and other personal effects as she entered the room. Her key was there, meaning it probably hadn't been stolen and used by anyone else—how would they have locked the door upon leaving?

Next to it was a larger tray that held an array of makeup, perfumes, and lotions for Agnes to apply just before leaving. Agnes enjoyed getting a variety of scents in pretty bottles and there were some new additions since the last time Pen was here.

The small entry way opened up to a single enormous room that was a combination sitting area, office, library, and bedroom, the latter separated by a large silk curtain rather than a wall. Agnes hadn't wanted the burden of wheeling herself through doors when she could make it as simple as wheeling herself from one part of the space to the other. Penelope thought it was all very novel and modern, reminding her of the lofts in Greenwich Village where poor artists were making their homes.

The walls were filled with vibrant paintings that lifted the spirit and made one feel carefree. Penelope cast only a passing glance over them in favor of more relevant things.

She couldn't help a lingering look over the sitting area in front of the fireplace. When Penelope had spent nights here in the past, Agnes and she had spent many an evening in front of that fireplace talking, mostly of memories of her mother. The only thing Penelope knew of her mother's past was that her estranged family was back in California. It was one thing her mother had been unwilling to ever discuss. Agnes had only been able to fill in small insignificant details that hinted at a troupe of entertainers, which Penelope found thrilling.

Penelope dismissed those memories to focus on her

mission at hand. She continued on to the curtained-off bedroom area. As Chives had indicated, the large bed was made, every pillow in place. No one would have suspected that someone had suffered in the throes of death only two nights ago.

Even after death, it was obvious to the observant eye that Agnes slept on the right side of the bed, nearest the window. The empty wheelchair was still there, and Penelope's eyes lingered on it for a long moment. Further evidence sat on the nightstand, which still held Agnes's reading glasses, hand lotion, and the small buzzer she used to call for either Beth or Chives.

The latest novel Agnes had been reading before bed also rested on the nightstand. Penelope peered in closer to see that it was an Agatha Christie novel, *The Man in the Brown Suit*.

A sad smile crept to Penelope's face as she picked up the book. Agatha Christie had only written a few books, and was probably known only to true lovers of mystery novels. This was a new one, which must have just recently been published. Even Penelope, for all her love of mysteries, hadn't read it yet.

Pen turned it to the back and scanned the description which promised yet another gripping mystery from the author. She flipped through the pages, wondering how far Agnes had read. Something about her dying before getting to the denouement saddened Pen. Then again, there was no bookmark, so perhaps she had finished it? She knew Agnes abhorred the idea of saving her place by turning the corners of pages, which ruined them.

"Where is the bookmark?"

"That was exactly what Miss Sterling asked that night. I searched for it but I couldn't find it. She was rather upset about that, as she had only just started the book, and had lost her place."

"Was it there Thursday night, the night before?"

"Yes, miss."

"And Friday night it was gone?"

"Yes, miss."

That was interesting, but Penelope wasn't sure how it was relevant.

"The one you saw Thursday night, was it gold with an imprint of a peacock?" Penelope had given it to Agnes for Christmas, a small trinket that she'd hoped reminded her of her time in India. It was only gold plated, so not expensive, but Agnes had loved it all the same.

"I believe so, Miss Banks."

That stung. Not only was Agnes dead, but the present she'd given her was missing as well.

But was it connected to her death?

Penelope worked her brain and couldn't figure out how it could be. She filed it away all the same. Perhaps some connection would come later on.

She opened the drawer to the nightstand and peered in. Inside were a notepad, pen, a handkerchief and the bell she used to use to call when she needed something and someone was close enough to hear it. Though it wasn't particularly orderly inside, nothing seemed amiss.

"Could you tell me about that night as you helped Agnes to bed?"

Beth nodded and proceeded. "After dinner, I accompanied her here. I ran the bath for her as always."

Penelope's eyes flicked to the door on the other side of the bed that led to Agnes's private bathroom. She took a bath every night before bedtime rather than in the morning. Penelope never understood why, in a world of French soaps and delightfully scented lotions and oils, Agnes insisted on plain, unscented Ivory soap. But Agnes explained that she enjoyed slipping into the freshly laundered sheets, changed every day, smelling fresh and clean.

"And she seemed her usual self?"

"Indeed," Beth confirmed with a nod. "After her bath, I helped her into her nightgown, then into bed. Once she was settled, I left, locking the door as usual when I did."

"And you never noticed the letter or the bottle of poison?"

"Not until the next morning," Beth said, the color draining from her face. The sight of Agnes that morning must have been quite disturbing.

"Was the room locked during the day?"

"No, though I thought perhaps it should have been."

"Oh?"

"Because of theft."

Beth must have been referring to the earrings Julia supposedly stole, and was being as tactful as Chives about it. *Someone* in the house had stolen them.

"But Miss Sterling didn't like having to carry her key around with her, or bother Chives and me with opening it for her." Beth sniffed as though remembering how considerate Agnes was.

"She didn't ring for you at all during the night?" Penelope asked, moving on.

"No," Beth said, beginning to show signs of despair. "I don't understand it. She didn't often ring during the night, but why wouldn't she have...?"

"We should test the system," Penelope announced.

"I beg your pardon?"

"Maybe someone did something so it wouldn't work. If

we can show that the call button wasn't working, that might be proof that she didn't commit suicide."

Beth perked up at that idea.

"Go to the staff area and listen for the call. I'll press the button from here."

"Yes, miss," Beth said before hurrying out.

Penelope waited the half a minute it would take Beth to get to the staff area before stabbing her thumb into the call button on Agnes's nightstand. She pressed multiple times just to make sure.

When Beth appeared a few minutes later, she could see the crestfallen look on her face.

"It worked perfectly," she said in a tone of resignation.

"So Agnes simply didn't call that night?" Penelope asked in saddened disbelief.

"It would seem so."

They both stood and let that fact sink in.

"I suppose that's all for now. Thank you, Beth."

"Of course, Miss Banks. Anything to help find out what happened, I am happy to help with. Miss Sterling was a fine woman, a pleasure to have served. I will miss her dearly."

"So will I," Penelope said with a sad smile. She walked out ahead of her, leaving Beth to close and lock the door behind them.

This had led to nothing but even more disappointing revelations.

Still, there was something that still nagged at Penelope, something Arabella had said. In her head, she replayed the conversation in the kitchen until she alighted upon what it was. Fortunately, it was a question that could be satisfied over lunch, which would be starting at any moment.

It was time to learn more about these guests of Agnes's.

CHAPTER SEVEN

Penelope went upstairs to collect Cousin Cordelia just in time for lunch to be announced. When they returned to the first floor they met the first of the other guests before even making it to the dining room.

He was an older gentleman, perhaps in his late forties or early fifties. The trim mustache, stern expression, and perfectly erect stance of his long body spoke to order and structure. No doubt Major Hallaway.

"Good afternoon," he said eyeing the cousin duo with an assessing gaze. "Major Colin Hallaway," he said, by way of introduction.

"Penelope Banks and this is my cousin, Cordelia Davies."

"I assume one or both of you have been named beneficiaries as well?"

Quite the abrupt question. It seemed the major was a fan of getting straight to the meat of the matter. A little too direct, even for Penelope's tastes. Still, it might make pressing him for information easier; no need to handle his sensibilities with kid gloves.

"I've come solely to offer my sympathies," Cousin Cordelia said with a note of reproach in her voice that Penelope admired.

"I on the other hand am apparently named in the will. Are you related to Agnes?" It was a safe introductory question, never mind that Penelope had already been apprised of his status earlier.

"I am—*was* Agnes's cousin on her mother's side, though we weren't very close. Nothing to do with the age difference, mind you." He did seem to be almost a decade younger than his recently deceased cousin. His manner, expression, and tone of voice hinted at disapproval regarding Agnes's lifestyle, which was no doubt where the true divide between them lay. "Still, family is family, I suppose."

Still, inheritance is inheritance, Penelope interpreted to herself.

"I'm sorry for your loss," she said, wide eyes offering an overtly sympathetic look.

"Er, yes, of course." He was clearly uncomfortable with anything approaching sympathy. "What with the accident and all, it's understandable she might have, ah, done herself in. I'm honestly surprised it took her this long, to be frank. Still, dammed shame what happened."

Penelope bit her tongue. People dealt with loss in different ways, and she couldn't fully expect everyone to express their sorrow in a tactful manner. After all, he did say he wasn't close to his cousin. Still, to talk about her in such a manner seemed tasteless.

"So, ah, how did *you* know Agnes?" he asked, once again studying Penelope with a keen gaze.

"I was a family friend," she replied, earning her a dubious look. She wasn't about to satisfy his curiosity by going into the details of how close a friend Agnes was. Agnes had many friends, so it was still a bit of a mystery even to Penelope as to why she had been chosen to be named in her will.

"A friend, hmm? Just how many other friends are there?" he grumbled, no doubt realizing that his cut of the kale might be more meager than he first assumed.

"Lovey, who are you talking to?" All heads turned at the sound of that nasally, overly effeminate voice.

A woman about twenty years his junior, with hair that would never pass muster as a natural shade of blonde, entered the foyer from the parlor. The dark green velvet dress she wore was beautiful and no doubt expensive, a sharp contrast to the major's plain, almost old-fashioned suit. Penelope had no idea what the major's financial situation was like, but if those pearls of hers were real, he could certainly afford to be less disgruntled about a *slightly* smaller share of Agnes's estate.

She floated in on a cloud of expensive perfume and the sort of self-confidence that could only come from usually getting what one wanted in life. She was naturally attractive in a way that didn't require the copious amounts of eyeliner and rouge she sported. As it was, the whole effect transformed her from pretty to somewhat vampy, which Pen suspected was exactly what she was aiming for. The way her eyes deliberately landed on the younger of the two cousins added a predatory tinge to the air between them.

She latched on to the arm of the major.

"I'm Lottie," she announced, making sure to give Penelope a level gaze. "The wife."

Major Hallaway, cleared his throat. "This is *Loretta* Hallaway," he corrected, apparently not enthusiastic about the shortened version.

Lottie laughed as though this was a constant, amusing battle they were used to fighting. It died quickly, replaced by a reptilian gaze that shifted back and forth between Penelope and Cordelia "So, which a you is in the will?"

Penelope was able to control herself a bit more than Cousin Cordelia, who squeaked out a breath of indignant shock at the forward question. The couple apparently had more in common with each other than a first glance might indicate. Neither one was strong on tact or manners.

"That would be me, Penelope Banks. It's very nice to meet you, Mrs. Hallaway."

"Miss Banks was apparently a friend of the family," said Major Hallaway. Pen noted his stress on the word "apparently." "And this is her chaperone, Mrs. Cordelia Davies."

Penelope bristled at the label. Obviously the major was stuck in a different era when a young woman couldn't so much as step foot outside the house without a matron attending to her. It made her all the more curious about his marriage to a woman who so obviously paid no attention to societal rules.

"Chaperone?" Lottie repeated casting a grin Penelope's way. "Does that mean you're a troublemaker?"

Penelope smiled despite herself. She decided she didn't entirely dislike the major's wife after all. Yes, Lottie was brash and aggressive, but Pen preferred people who spoke their minds to those who hid behind keeping up appearances. It would certainly make her investigation easier.

"Perhaps we should head to the dining room," Major Hallaway said, already corralling his wife that way.

"Well, I never..." Cousin Cordelia softly breathed out in a huff in their wake.

"This should be an interesting lunch," Penelope whispered with a bemused smile as she watched the couple go ahead of them.

In the dining room, an older woman in a light blue dress had arrived before all of them. She stood in quiet contemplation, looking out at the water through the windows.

When she turned to greet them Penelope noted how, somewhat like Cousin Cordelia, she had a preference for a style that didn't try to keep up with modern trends. The two women were around the same age but her clothing wasn't *quite* as old-fashioned as her Cousin Cordelia's. The draped waist was paired with a tonneau skirt billowing out into an egg shape that had been all the rage just after the Great War. Once an unabashed lover of modern fashion, Penelope noted how stylish this particular style would have been at the time. In fact, for a woman her age, she dressed in a decidedly youthful manner, which Penelope admired.

She recognized her face from Agnes's Fourth of July party, even though she'd only seen her from a distance. This one had been rather indulgent with both the gin and the desserts, mostly sitting out the festivities to observe rather than participate. The fact that Agnes had never bothered to introduce her was odd, considering she had been named in the will, so she was presumably a close friend.

"Mrs. Mayweather, I presume?" Penelope decided to forgo the pretense of not knowing who anyone was. Lunch would only last so long and she didn't want to bother with drawn-out introductions.

"Yes," Mrs. Mayweather replied, scrutinizing Penelope with mild surprise. Her hand rose to her chest to fiddle with the front of her dress. "I'm afraid I don't recall being introduced."

"I apologize. No, we've never been formally introduced, but I do recognize you from one of Agnes's parties."

"That's our Penelope," Cousin Cordelia said proudly. "She can remember absolutely anything. Ask her to read a line from a page in any book she's ever read and she'll recite it perfectly! Very strange really, but it has saved me more than a few times when I've misplaced something."

"I see," Mrs. Mayweather said in a distracted way as she gave Penelope an uncertain look. Penelope could understand her wariness. The way her cousin had described her, it seemed as though she suffered some strange mental disorder. "Forgive me, but I'm not quite as good at remembering faces."

"There were always far too many people at Agnes's parties. I'm Penelope Banks, a friend of hers."

"And I'm Cordelia Davies, Penelope's cousin joining her. It's so nice to meet you." Penelope could hear the slightly fawning intonation in her cousin's voice. She had obviously found an acceptable peer amid the current cast of questionable characters.

"Iris Mayweather." Her face settled into something slightly more pleasant as she addressed Cousin Cordelia. "I'm one of Agnes's oldest and dearest friends, since childhood in fact."

"Really, how fascinating," Penelope remarked, suddenly interested. She would love to hear stories about Agnes's childhood over lunch, though not before she addressed other more pressing topics.

Major Hallaway took the liberty of sitting at the head of the table. Lottie sat next to him. The table normally sat sixteen. With only five present, it behooved the rest of them to take up seats on either side nearest him to avoid any awkward distances.

Mrs. Mayweather sat on his other side and Cousin Cordelia happily took up the seat next to her. That left

Penelope to sit next to Lottie to even things out, which she wasn't opposed to even if it meant she'd spend the rest of the day smelling like a Turkish incense market.

"It must have been quite the unpleasant shock to have been visiting the very night that Agnes...passed away," Penelope began, feeling no need for idle niceties. She was still curious about something Arabella had said and needed her thoughts satisfied about the matter.

Cousin Cordelia cast a thoroughly disapproving look her way, but Penelope kept her eyes locked on the two sitting at the opposite corner of the table, Mrs. Mayweather and Major Hallaway.

"It was dammed inconsiderate if you ask me. Pardon my language." The major flashed a brief, apologetic look in the direction of the older women seated with them. He turned back to Penelope with his brow once again furrowed. "I must say, she certainly wasn't the gracious hostess that she's so often lauded as being. In fact, she seemed rather put out by our arrival, despite it being *her* request for us to visit. Then, after making a point of inviting us to stay for the week, she decides to pull this nonsense? It certainly speaks to something being not quite right with the old gal. I suppose she wanted to send a message of some kind, or perhaps make her goodbyes before she ended it all. She could have at least waited until we'd driven back home. To be questioned by the police in that manner, as though we were suspects! Never mind my being a serving member of the United States military."

Once again Penelope had to bite her tongue. Still, he had satisfied her curiosity about what was bothering her. Arabella had mentioned that some of the guests were a surprise this week and Major Hallaway had confirmed that,

COLETTE CLARK

despite this supposed invitation, it had come as a surprise to Agnes as well.

So what were they doing here? And who had invited them? Was this invitation simply a ruse to be here unannounced? All to kill Agnes and make it look like a suicide?

The questions were getting rather fanciful at this point. Still, Penelope didn't dismiss the idea.

"Don't get yourself all worked up, lovey," Lottie cooed, reaching out to affectionally stroke his arm. He visibly melted under her touch. "After all, she did leave us a little somethin' in the will didn't she? I'd say that makes it pretty considerate of her, especially seein' as how we was already here and all."

The frank reproach with which the two older women seated across the table regarded Lottie would have had Penelope laughing to herself if the context hadn't been so offensive.

"Yes, I suppose that was convenient," Penelope said tersely. "Unless you already live nearby?"

"I'm stationed in Washington D.C." Major Hallaway stated.

"But who knows? Maybe now, with all this money we're gettin', we'll be allowed to move back to New York again," Lottie said hopefully.

Penelope now understood the accent that seemed to slip through every so often. Lottie was a bona fide New Yorker, the type Pen was used to finding in speakeasies rather than 5th Avenue mansions.

"I don't think so, Loretta dear."

Ignoring both Lottie's pout and Cousin Cordelia's admonishing gaze, Penelope continued with her inquiry. "Did you often visit Agnes here in Long Island? Or perhaps her apartment in Manhattan?"

62

"Manhattan? Like those fancy buildings near Central Park?" Lottie asked, perking up.

"We most certainly did not," Major Hallaway answered in a tone that indicated he would die before visiting such a locale.

"I for one don't understand why she invited us here when there was nothin' fun goin' on," Lottie whined. "I keep hearin' about all these parties she throws but when we gets here, it's nothin' but dull, dull, dull. Thank goodness I got to drive into the city every once in a while. And at least she had some decent hooch on hand."

Major Hallaway cleared his throat in such an aggressive way that most of his table companions started. Lottie just giggled.

"When did you last visit Agnes?" Penelope asked.

"Late last summer," Lottie answered. She jerked her chin up toward Mrs. Mayweather. "You were here, remember? In fact, it was a week before—"

"What matters now is that we were at least able to visit with her before her death," Major Hallaway said, interrupting his wife. "The only thing left to do is get this business with the will over with and return to Washington where I can resume my duties with the government."

It wasn't lost on Penelope that Major Hallaway had deliberately cut his wife off. She wanted to pry a bit more as she'd been certain Lottie was about to say that they'd been here just before Agnes's accident. It was irrelevant to the matter at hand so, rather than press the issue, she decided to shift to another topic she was curious about.

"Had Agnes seemed melancholy, or worried about something this week? Was there any indication that she wanted to end it all?" Anyone who answered in the affirmative would rise to the top of her suspect list unless they had a valid reason why they would think such a thing.

Before anyone could so much as react to the question, they were interrupted by their final guest of the day.

"Well, it seems we have ourselves a party."

CHAPTER EIGHT

Everyone at the dining table for lunch turned to view their latest guest. The man standing in the archway leading to the room was young, tall, and quite handsome in a rakish sort of way.

It wasn't so much his features as the way he carried himself: hair parted in the middle and swept back; eyes amused but with a hint of calculating design and impishness; cleft chin lifted just a bit, to the point of confidence rather than haughtiness.

This guest, Penelope did recognize and remember quite well: Raymond Colley.

Unlike Mrs. Mayweather, Agnes needn't have introduced Raymond at any of her parties. He had made himself known to every young, eligible, somewhat attractive female in attendance. And many a young female had certainly made their affections quite clear in return. Penelope hadn't been lured in, having learned her lesson with Clifford. Once Raymond had learned she was a veritable pauper, his interest had cooled to mere politeness, mostly upon realizing she was still a favorite of his aunt's.

As questionable a gentleman as he was, Penelope was glad to have another younger person in attendance, especially one so contrarian when it came to "propriety and decorum." Lottie was amusing but probably couldn't provide much in the way of information. At least Raymond had spent more than a week in Agnes's presence.

He was dressed quite fashionably in a tailored navy jacket and Oxford bags, trousers done in the current trending style of a much wider leg. She noted, in particular, the Patek Philippe watch on his wrist as he removed his hat. That was certainly a rare and expensive thing. Pen had once seen it on a man she'd played cards with. Before she'd taken him for almost two hundred dollars, he'd bragged about the obscene cost of it.

If Raymond could afford to throw money away on a watch like that Agnes's allowance must have been generous. Most of the bond boys on Wall Street barely made a middle-class income, simply idling their time in a profession that was socially acceptable while their family money covered their lavish tastes.

A smile broadened his mouth as his eyes landed on Penelope. She could see why Arabella giggled like a schoolgirl at the mere mention of his name. He certainly was charming in his own way.

"My dear Miss Penelope Banks, what a delightful surprise to find you here," he said in a voice which she was certain was shamelessly practiced.

"Good day, Mr. Colley," Penelope replied in a perfectly neutral tone. Today of all days was certainly not the occasion for flirtation.

"I believe I've been introduced to everyone else." He looked around with sardonic amusement, briefly lingering on Lottie long enough to have Major Hallaway clearing his throat. Raymond rounded the table to take the seat next to Cousin Cordelia. "But who is this lovely creature?"

God bless her, Penelope's cousin managed a blush even as she looked on in disapproval. "I'm Penelope's *older* cousin."

"Her chaperone," Lottie teased.

"Chaperone?" Raymond repeated, brow raised. He turned to give Penelope a daring look. "Ah yes, our Pen is known to get up to a bit of trouble, isn't she?"

Penelope glared at him, which caused him to laugh.

"So lovely to see the rest of you, *yet again*," Raymond said, looking around once more with a grin on his face.

Penelope studied the reactions of everyone else at the table. Lottie was positively kittenish. Major Hallaway was understandably aggravated. Mrs. Mayweather's lips pursed with displeasure.

"My sympathies for the loss of your aunt," Penelope said in a pointed way.

"Yes, it was rather tragic," he replied with an exaggerated sigh. "Still, I am pleased she thought of me when she was jotting down the old will."

"I understand you were here the night she died? Quite late, after everyone else had turned in?" Penelope was pleased to find that she had finally managed to crack his facade of playing the Lothario.

"I'm usually here every weekend visiting my aunt," he said with a hint of defensiveness.

"Not just the weekends," she heard Mrs. Mayweather say through her pursed lips.

The moment was interrupted by Chives asking if they would like something to drink.

"I know dear old Agnes has at least a few bottles of bubbly rolling around here somewhere. Good old Barney

COLETTE CLARK

never let her down. Why not toast to her memory!"
Raymond announced.

It was very much an unpopular proposal.

"I hardly think that's appropriate," Mrs. Mayweather
chided.

"You *are* aware of the current federal laws against that
sort of thing, I presume?" Major Hallaway asked, giving him
a hard look.

"I think it's a swell idea. If anything calls for breaking
the law, I'd say it's this," Lottie countered, giving Raymond
a flattering smile.

"Au contraire," Raymond said, lifting a finger in the air.
"It's only illegal to *sell*, not *imbibe*. Besides, dear old Agnes
wouldn't want it to go to waste."

Next to Raymond, Cousin Cordelia began wringing her
hands with dismay. Penelope hoped she didn't inadvertently call for her medicine.

As far as Penelope was concerned she was always in the
mood for champagne, and Agnes certainly had the best. She
knew full well Agnes would have wanted them to raise a
glass to her, even considering the circumstances of her
death. However, unlike Raymond, she wasn't quite tactless
enough to announce such a thing in present company.
Besides, she wanted to be sober and clear-headed during
lunch. Bubbles had a way of going straight to her brain,
making it loose and muddled.

"I will have lemonade," Mrs. Mayweather said with a
firm nod.

"Oh, that sounds lovely," Cousin Cordelia said, grateful
that more moralistic minds had prevailed. "I'll have the
same."

"I'll have lemonade as well," Penelope said, earning her
a look of extreme disappointment from Raymond.

"I'll take that champagne, Chives," he said.

"A ginger ale for my wife and me," Major Hallaway instructed.

"I think I'll have some of that champagne too," Lottie insisted, scowling at her husband.

"Loretta!" he hissed.

"Raymond is right, it ain't illegal—*isn't* illegal," she corrected with a guilty smile.

Chives waited patiently for a final decision.

"Champagne," Lottie confirmed, casting a quick vicious look toward her husband before planting a satisfied smile on her face. His jaw tightened, but he remained silent.

Chives escaped to retrieve their drinks.

"I was just asking about Agnes's disposition this past week," Penelope resumed. "The last time I saw her she'd been in such good spirits. Of course that was over New Year's. Did she seem at all blue to you this week?"

"Ah, I see," Raymond said with an arched eyebrow and a wry smile. "You want to know if dear old auntie gave any glaring hints regarding her looming demise?"

"I wouldn't have put it quite so bluntly," Penelope said in a terse voice. "This is hardly an amusing matter."

"Oh come now, Agnes of all people would want us to have a good laugh."

"Agnes certainly had a sense of humor, but I doubt very much it extended to her own death," Penelope replied.

"And why not? She was always one to laugh at herself. The very fact that she did it her way, speaks to the notion that she'd want us to, I dunno, celebrate it? The only wonder is that she did it in such an uninspired manner. Usually she's the eccentric type."

"Unless it wasn't done by her," Penelope retorted in anger, instantly regretting it. If the killer was sitting at this table, she didn't want to give them any warning that she was on to them.

Chives returned with their drinks, and no doubt felt the weight of the silence in the room as he placed them before each guest.

"Are you suggesting there was foul play involved?" Major Hallaway asked once he had gone.

"I'm saying," Penelope began, taking a breath to calm herself, "That Agnes is the last person on earth I'd suspect of suicide. Anyone who actually knew her would agree with me."

"Ohh, murder," Lottie said, eyes wide with the thrill of that suggestion.

"Penelope dear, perhaps not during lunch," Cousin Cordelia said, fanning herself.

"That's outrageous! And frankly, I don't care for the accusatory tone," the major said, giving her a hard stare.

"And I don't care for the complete and utter lack of regard for her memory. You sit here eating lunch and drinking her champagne," Penelope cast a quick baleful look toward Raymond then turned back to the major, "all while no doubt calculating just how much of her fortune you'll be receiving."

"I am not a murderer!" he practically roared. Even Lottie shrank away from it.

"Ditto for me. The bond business has been booming," Raymond said, seemingly amused at the direction the conversation had taken. "Besides, I always heard that poison was a dame's choice of bumping someone off. Isn't that the story? Maybe it was one of the chickadees here at the table." He waggled his eyes at Lottie and Penelope, then turned to Mrs. Mayweather. "Or fussy old hens."

"I beg your pardon?" Mrs. Mayweather exclaimed, positively livid.

"I've had just about enough from you, young man!" Major Hallaway raged.

"Well, *I* certainly had no reason to kill her. I'm not even a relative. Frankly, I'm rather surprised to be included in the will at all," Mrs. Mayweather said, indignation filling her voice.

"Oh," Cousin Cordelia cried out. "My medicine!"

"The fact of the matter is, the police have done their due diligence and come to the *correct* conclusion that it was suicide. Casting such aspersions is a dangerous game, young lady," the major said, giving Penelope a dark look.

Suddenly, Penelope had no appetite either for the food or the company. "I'm going to get some fresh air," she said by way of excusing herself. She rose up to leave just as lunch was brought in.

Penelope rushed upstairs to retrieve her hooded coat and put on winter shoes, then came back down to exit through the French doors. Even in winter, the grounds were perfect for strolling and thinking. The snow had been shoveled off the various pathways that led to the gardens, swimming pool, tennis courts, and other areas on the estate, all of them dead or winterized. The cold air cleared her mind and she mentally revisited everything said over her brief attendance at lunch.

Perhaps Cousin Cordelia had been right about her meddling. Pen had been rather tactless. Raymond had just upset her so with his blithe attitude, as though Agnes's death were nothing more than an humorous tale to recount at future parties. Perhaps he was just giddy over the prospect of no longer being limited to whatever allowance

Agnes had been giving him. He now potentially had access to the whole kit and caboodle.

Of course, Major Hallaway and Lottie had been no less mercenary about their hopes for what the will would reveal.

Mrs. Mayweather was still a bit of a mystery, but she'd been awfully defensive about not being the murderer. Then again, Penelope wasn't sure how she'd react if someone had accused her.

Penelope realized she'd have to be far more subtle than she'd been at lunch if she was going to get answers. That had been terrifically disastrous and already had her fellow guests viewing her with wary regard, if not outright resentment.

The same headstrong young woman who liked to butt heads with her father had gotten her exactly the same results they had in the past: absolutely nothing.

It would seem that acting the sleuth required the kind of finesse she used during her card games. The men she played with had a habit of taking her for an easy mark, and she'd been happy to let them think that. Even as she won, she'd made a show of innocent surprise at her dumb luck, at least until they finally caught on, at which point she usually had all the money she needed.

That was it! She'd have to treat this all like a game of cards. Tonight, she'd make her apologies and blame it on some silly affectation that people often ascribed to hysterical women. Lottie would probably be the only one who wouldn't buy it. Still, she'd watch, listen, and pay close attention to the other players, homing in on any bit of evidence dealt out.

By dinner tonight, Penelope would be playing a whole different game, and she wouldn't fail.

CHAPTER NINE

THAT EVENING PENELOPE HEADED DOWN EARLY BEFORE dinner, wanting to take advantage of the bar in the parlor room. When playing cards, she'd always had a glass of something to help loosen her up. Since her new strategy entailed mimicking those heady nights in speakeasies and clubs, she thought she'd make herself something to set the proper mood.

The house had been built long before the days of Prohibition but Agnes certainly hadn't bothered to upgrade the parlor accordingly. The bar stretched the length of the long room. Behind it, chrome and glass shelves were filled with various spirits and wines to accommodate even the most eccentric tastes.

Penelope wasn't surprised to find Raymond already availing himself of a bottle. She paused, wondering how best to approach him with an olive branch.

Fortunately, Raymond didn't seem to be the type to hold grudges. "Oh come now, Miss Banks, let's be friends," he said, his back still turned to her, though he could see her in the mirror-backed bar. "At least allow me to make you a cocktail by way of a peace offering."

"I can make my own, thank you," she said as she neared the bar.

"Worried I may try to poison you?" He asked with a chuckle, turning around to give her a wink.

"Your little jokes about this are tiresome," she said, though she made sure to keep her tone light-hearted.

"Then, allow me to wake you up. You look like a bee's knees kinda gal."

She realized that allowing him to make her drink might be a way to ward off his concerns that she might suspect him. "Fine, but I'll take a gin rickey instead."

"Atta girl!" he said cheerfully.

Penelope did make sure to watch closely as he made it. It didn't hurt to be prudent. She was sure it was Chives who instructed that there should be limes and lemons made available tonight, knowing at least a few guests would indulge. Having worked for a woman like Agnes, he would have had to have an open mind about such things. Pen grabbed one of the limes to top off her drink.

"So, do you really suspect murder?" Raymond asked.

"We probably shouldn't have a repeat of what happened at lunch. Tonight I think it would be best to celebrate Agnes's life, not her death." All the better to find out just how close everyone was to her and what their motives might be.

"Chin chin to that," he said, lifting his glass in salute.

"I hate to interrupt," Lottie said, announcing herself. They both turned to greet her.

She was wearing a red silky number better suited for a party in the wee hours than the dinner prior to the reading of a will. She had, for some reason, thrown a mink shawl on as well. Penelope at least had the grace to wear a simple black dress tonight.

Lottie slinked her way in, a coy smirk on her lips as though she'd caught them doing something they shouldn't. She settled next to Penelope, again in a cloud of expensive musk, causing her to wonder if Lottie practiced temperance in any area of her life.

"I'll take a white lady," she ordered, giving Raymond an expectant look.

Raymond's brow rose but he grinned and set his drink down to get started on it. "It seems chivalry isn't dead after all," he muttered.

Penelope favored their third party with her attention. "I was curious as to how you and the major met. I'm sure it's a romantic story."

She gave Penelope a sardonic look as though she was fooling no one with that quaint phrasing. "It actually *was* the sweetest thing. I was getting roughed up by the fuzz, and what does lovey do but step right in and rescue me, just like one of those knights in a fairy tale. He took me out to get a coffee, seeing as how I was, um, all shook up. He's been spoiling me ever since," she smiled and shrugged, showing off the mink as though to prove that point.

"The fuzz, you say? What could a decent lady such as yourself have been doing to invite harassment from the police?" Raymond asked with mock earnestness.

Now, he was the one getting the sardonic look. "Minding my own business is what."

Raymond laughed.

Penelope regarded him with curious amusement. He did have a way of lightening the mood. She didn't miss the way he'd caught on to "the fuzz" so easily. Even Penelope, with her secret criminal life, had only recently learned that bit of slang, which she was pretty sure wasn't used in the common vernacular.

"Mmm," Lottie said, sipping her drink. "This takes me back to my days in New York. I always knew exactly where to get the best booze in town. D.C. is so stuffy and lovey never lets me have that kind of fun anymore."

"Here's to Agnes and her non-stuffy supply of the best booze in town," Raymond said, lifting his glass once again. He winked at Penelope. "Pen and I have decided to become friends. Perhaps you'd like to join our trio of magnanimity?"

"Magna-what?" Lottie asked with a frown.

Raymond chuckled softly, realizing he wasn't dealing with an intellectual. "Let's just call it a *ménage à trois.*"

That was a term Lottie apparently understood, which was not a surprise to either of the other two. She smirked and coyly sipped her drink.

Penelope sighed and wandered away, wondering how many drinks Raymond had already had prior to her arrival. He was hopeless as far as holding a serious conversation.

"I suppose that leaves us two lovebirds," Raymond lamented, then joined Lottie when she giggled.

Penelope focused her attention on one of the many paintings in the room. It was a Henri Matisse. Agnes had loved his more abstract work and this one—

She stopped, her brow wrinkling in concentration as she moved closer to study the work of art. Something was off. Her eyes scanned the piece, comparing it to the one in her memory from when Agnes had first shown her the painting.

"Gadzooks," she muttered aloud.

"Don't start claiming the goods yet, Pen, the will doesn't

get read until tomorrow," Raymond called out. She heard Lottie giggle again.

"This is a fake," she announced.

"A what now?" he asked, uncertainty coloring his voice.

Penelope turned around to face the other two who had paused mid-drink. "It's a fake! This painting isn't the original."

"You're crackers," Raymond said, but he was quick to round the bar and head her way along with Lottie. He leaned in, his eyes narrowed with speculation. "How can you even tell?"

"It looks like a mess to me," Lottie said, her face scrunched with skepticism.

"I know what this painting is supposed to look like. Even if I didn't, yes it *appears* to be the original, but peer in closer to the right-hand corner."

The other two both leaned in even closer, squinting in a way that would be comical under any other circumstance. Their eyes went wide as they both noted the tiny little scribble, no bigger than a sunflower seed, painted in black.

"Is that a...?" Lottie began.

Raymond finished, practically coughing it out, "a damned rat!"

"No, it's a mouse," Lottie said, squinting again.

"Either way, as far as I know, Matisse isn't known for such a cheeky addition to his work," Penelope pointed out.

Lottie pulled back and gave Penelope a haughty look. "How do you know it wasn't just added on later by some jokester?"

"No doubt some drunken prank committed during one of her parties," Raymond answered, still frowning with dismay as he stared at the painting. He turned to Penelope. "That explains it. It's the real painting with nothing more than a simple job for a restorer to take care of and there you are."

"Not so simple, I'm afraid. The stroke of paint over the tiny tail portion. See here?" Penelope pointed to the incriminating clue. "Whoever reproduced the original got that stroke right, to a nearly identical degree. But it's a stroke that lies on top of the mouse or rat tail. Either a reckless oversight or they intended it." She pulled back and her eyes roamed across the rest of the painting. "There are other telling differences as well. Minor, but it would be obvious to the original artist."

"One would have thought you'd painted it yourself, you know so much about it," Lottie scoffed.

"No, I just have a memory like, well like a painting. One that captures everything. And this is most certainly not the painting that was hanging here when Agnes first bought it."

"Well, that's a fine thing, ain't it?" Lottie said, her hand resting on one hip jerked to the side. "What else in this place is a fake?"

"A good question," Penelope's eyes roamed the room to inspect the other artwork. On the walls throughout the mansion hung paintings and drawings from artists Agnes had taken a liking to, both world-renowned names and those whose careers had started and ended in Greenwich Village.

"What question is that?" Major Hallaway asked entering the room to join them. His brow furrowed in irritation at the sight of Lottie with a drink in her hand.

"Pen here thinks this painting is a fake," Raymond said.

"It's got a mouse!" Lottie exclaimed, stabbing one finger toward it.

"I beg your pardon?" That was enough to draw his attention away from his cocktail-sipping wife and directly to the painting next to her.

"Come see for yourself."

The major walked over and leaned in. He made a disgruntled sound before straightening back up. "Well now, this is a very serious thing. I'm going to demand an immediate accounting for all items of any value on this property."

"Maybe Auntie Agnes wasn't as well-off as she wanted us to believe. She may have sold the original, and replaced it with this hoping no one would notice." Raymond suggested. "Come tomorrow, we may find out she didn't have two nickels to rub together." He grinned into his drink at the stir this caused, but Penelope could see the slight wrinkle of worry in his brow.

"As far as I can tell, the other paintings in the room, even those worth far more, are the originals. Not that Matisse was anything to dismiss. Someone made a nice bit of green from selling the original," Penelope said.

"And just how would you know?" Major Hallaway asked, casting a suspicious gaze her way.

"I'm an expert," Penelope said, leaving it ambiguous rather than explain her condition once again. It did nothing to soften his distrustful look, but the way his eyes darted to the painting indicated he was far more concerned about this development.

"See? No need to worry, that leaves plenty of kale for us other, *ahem*, rats to nibble on," Raymond said, lifting his glass in salute.

Everyone ignored him, by now used to his enjoyment of causing trouble.

Penelope considered the painting once again. Of all the artwork, at least in this room, it would have been the easiest to reproduce if someone was inclined to steal the original and make money at the same time. Still, it did raise all sorts of questions. Why had they left the rat-or-mouse as a give-away? Had Agnes sold the original or had someone else stolen and replaced it? What other paintings from Agnes's impressive collection had been reproduced?

Certainly some of these could be answered by Mr. Wilcox tomorrow when he came to read the will. If Agnes was in enough financial trouble to sell one of her beloved paintings, it made Pen wonder what surprises would be in store.

Cousin Cordelia arrived with Mrs. Mayweather, the two of them chatting like schoolgirls.

"I see we're all gathered with our pre-dinner delights," Cousin Cordelia said, pursing her lips at the drinks in certain guests' hands. Penelope caught her casting a quick, longing gaze toward the bar, no doubt wondering if she should pre-medicate before their meal, considering how the last one ended.

"It turns out one of us has been robbed!" Raymond announced with such dramatic flair it caused both of the newest arrivals to blink rapidly. He thrust a pointed finger at the painting. "This, as it turns out, is a fake!"

Both women flashed their gazes to the painting. The subsequent expressions of puzzlement on their faces made Penelope think they would have their doubts about it even if it wasn't a fake. Modern art wasn't for everyone.

"Nothing we can do about it tonight of course," Major Hallaway said, his face still a picture of consternation. "But rest assured I will be taking this up with Mr. Wilcox tomorrow."

Penelope thought perhaps that might be best. Men had a habit of disregarding the claims of women. Seeing as how Mr. Wilcox had decided her estranged father was the best person to relate the news regarding Agnes's death, he was most likely some bluenosed old man who would think Penelope was some senseless, silly girl. He'd listen if Major Hall-away was the one to address the issue.

"My goodness," Cousin Cordelia said, already fretting as she turned to Mrs. Mayweather. "First your earrings, Iris, now this?"

"So the maid's an art thief to boot?" Lottie said with a sharp laugh.

"Lottie please," Major Hallaway hissed.

Apparently everyone was aware of Julia's theft, Penelope noted.

"My door was locked at all times," Mrs. Mayweather huffed. "She must have been *some kind* of professional."

"Nonsense, anyone can pick a lock." Lottie offered with a half-cocked smile of amusement.

"I doubt the two crimes are related," Major Hallaway said. "Thieves don't often change their modus operandi."

Chives made an appearance to announce that dinner was ready. Penelope wondered how much he had over-heard. The way his eyes darted to the Matisse, followed by a brief flash of concern caused a needle of worry to thread through her nerves. Penelope wasn't sure if Agnes would have confided any money concerns to him, but a good butler of the house always knew. His expression was most certainly tinged with surprise, meaning he had no idea the painting was a fake.

It made Penelope wonder what other mysteries she would unearth before the will was read tomorrow.

CHAPTER TEN

As it turned out, Mrs. Mayweather was the most talkative of all the guests in attendance at dinner. It made Penelope regret leaving so early from lunch. Who knew what she may have learned? But now it seemed that she would be able to make up for what she'd missed.

They were all seated in the same configuration they had been for lunch, with Major Hallaway at the head of the table. The soup course had only just been served and Mrs. Mayweather was regaling them with tales from the childhood she shared with Agnes.

"...of course Leticia had been the one to start it all, picking on poor Rebecca. I thought it awfully cruel to steal her shoes, forcing her to go home in her stockinged feet. Then to blame Agnes purely out of spite!" Mrs. Mayweather shook her head with dismay. "But she and Leticia had always been at odds with one another, and unfortunately dear Agnes did have a history of playing a prank or two herself. Thus, it was no wonder Miss Warren believed Leticia when she pointed the finger at Agnes as the culprit. Agnes of course protested to no avail."

Across from Penelope, Cousin Cordelia tutted in admonishment. Pen was rapt with attention, already picturing what devious retaliation the Agnes she'd known and loved would have devised against this Leticia. Even Raymond leaned in with interest awaiting the reveal.

"Obviously Agnes couldn't leave it at that. She took a pair of scissors to several of Leticia's locks. As for Miss Warren, she slathered ink across her chair, ruining her skirt for the rest of the day once she unknowingly sat down."

Penelope snickered, earning her a look of rebuke from Cousin Cordelia who found no humor in the act of petty revenge. Next to her, Raymond grinned.

"For that little act, Agnes was suspended from school, which she had no regrets about. I don't think she particularly enjoyed the structure of a classroom setting." Mrs. Mayweather looked around at the elegant dining room. "But she obviously never suffered for it."

"I'll say," Lottie said with a chuckle. She lifted the spoon in front of her and flicked a finger at it. "These things here? Pure silver. You know how much that goes for?"

"No need to interrupt for such a tasteless observation, Loretta," Major Hallaway said, staring at his wife the same way Penelope's father had cast his eyes upon her often enough.

Mrs. Mayweather stared down at her own spoon with interest and idly fingered it. Penelope noted that, unlike Cousin Cordelia, she wore no wedding ring. "I suppose this long after the fact even Leticia might look back and laugh about it all. She certainly wasn't laughing when she came to school the next day, her hair even shorter than yours is now, Miss Banks. Back then, it most definitely wasn't the style of the day. I myself would have never been so daring as to cut another girl's hair," Mrs. Mayweather said, briefly lowering her eyelids in a demure fashion. "But Agnes had no fear... God rest her soul."

"Who knew the old gal had a bit of mischief in her?" Raymond said, lifting his drink in approval. "I suppose my mother was the white sheep of the family."

"I recall murmurs about what a mischief-maker Agnes had been growing up. This certainly confirms it," Major Hallaway grumbled.

"I for one approve. Bullies shouldn't be allowed to get away with their misdeeds."

"For heaven's sake, Penelope," Cousin Cordelia chastised.

"She's young and full of vigor, just as we all were at that age," Mrs. Mayweather said, casting an indulgent smile Penelope's way. "Of course we had to grow out of it early if we wanted to catch a husband. Modern women have so many options. I'm a widow who has no intention of remarrying. Michael is the only man I've ever truly loved."

"Of course," Cousin Cordelia sympathized, patting her arm. Obviously the two of them had become quite close over the course of the day.

"Still, it is rather liberating in a way. No more fawning affectations to men, fancy perfumes and silly dresses, stuffing oneself into suffocating bindings—though I suppose in this day and age such things are no longer necessary."

"So, you and Agnes kept in touch all these years?" Penelope asked, hoping to learn more.

"Only recently. Early last year, I suddenly received a letter from her, even though we'd lost touch some time ago. From there we corresponded regularly. I had moved to Texas with my husband you see, the oil business. With the advancement of cars and planes, he's done quite well over the past decade. It was when he died last year that dear

Agnes reached out, offering her condolences. That one simple gesture, it made me long for home. Once I'd settled all my affairs down in Texas I returned early in the summer last year. It almost felt like Agnes and I were back in school again, young and carefree...despite her condition."

"Agnes was younger than her years," Penelope remarked. "Though I'm sure she enjoyed having you around as a reminder of that period of her life."

"She did dedicate a significant portion of our correspondence reminiscing about those days. I have them up in my room. I would bring them for us to laugh over. Still, I hate to think that longing for a simpler time may have contributed to her discontentment."

"I doubt it. Agnes had her eye firmly directed ahead, filled with optimism about the future," Penelope assured her. "She was very much a fan of the modern era. She only ever communicated by telephone with me. When they first became popular, she was thrilled at the idea of owning one. Her home was one of the first in Long Island to have one, even when she had no one else to call."

"Hmm, I've always been a fan of written correspondence. There's something rather more personal about writing and receiving a letter, don't you think?"

"I heartily agree," Cousin Cordelia said. "In our day, one had to take their time with things, it made you appreciate it more. Today it's all telephones, moving pictures, and *motorized* cars. The world is just buzzing by in a blur, I can hardly keep up."

"Yes, yes, I'm terrible when it comes to technology and modern life, so much of it is rather confusing. I realize certain advancements are inevitable, but the art of writing letters shouldn't disappear. Wouldn't you agree, Major?" Mrs. Mayweather said, turning her attention toward Major

Hallaway. "Your invitation to visit was also a handwritten letter, was it not?"

"Yes, but a telephone call would have most certainly sufficed. I see nothing wrong with that sort of progress in the world. Technology and methods of communication should move forward. In other areas," he cast a pointed look at Raymond, then Penelope, "I think our elders have it correct. Not everything in society needs changing."

"Oh lovey, don't be such a bluenose. After all, you married me didn't you?" Lottie said with a teasing smile.

"A marriage that is no doubt quite electrifying," Raymond said, waggling his eyebrows. It elicited exactly the sort of reaction he'd been hoping for. Both Mrs. Mayweather and Cousin Cordelia pursed their lips with distaste. Lottie giggled. Major Hallaway blustered with irritation. Penelope rolled her eyes. Every bit of it made Raymond laugh.

"As for me, I'm all about modernity. I hear you'll soon hear the actors talk in moving pictures, and after that it will probably be in color instead of black and white. Heck, it'll be no different than looking at me right across from you here at this table. And cars? They're only going to go faster. I, for one, can't wait. Here's hoping dear Auntie Agnes left me the Rolls in the will," he said with a grin, causing yet another stir.

"Well, you certainly seem to know *your* modern technology," Mrs. Mayweather commented, she turned to bless Major Hallaway with a smile. "And you, Major, I'd forgotten you were in army intelligence. Of course such things would appeal to you."

Major Hallaway seemed put out by this acknowledgment. "My activities in the military are not suitable for civilians, thank you."

"Well, I'm not one for reading letters. I'm a lover, not a reader," Lottie chimed in with a wink. "I don't even like books. I couldn't even tell you who's a popular writer these days."

No one seemed surprised by this announcement.

"Mrs. Mayweather, do you have any more stories from your childhood with Agnes? I think tonight would be a perfect time to hear them."

She flashed a grateful smile toward Penelope. "Of course, dear."

As the soup bowls were removed in anticipation of the next course, she told more stories of her schoolgirl days. At least for tonight, Penelope would focus on Agnes's life rather than her death. Tomorrow would be the reading of the will and she had a feeling that the current spirit of good-will would disappear under the lure of greed.

CHAPTER ELEVEN

THE MULTI-COURSE DINNER, ACCOMPANIED BY SEVERAL glasses of wine should have been enough ammunition to put Penelope into a deep sleep. Still, it eluded her. After taking a respite during dinner, her determination to learn more about Agnes's death had come roaring back.

She walked over to the window seat and sat down, wrapping her arms around her bent legs and resting her chin on her knees as she stared out into the night. The moon was nearly full but fell behind the house so it cast a dark shadow that reached almost to the edge of the terrace. Beyond that, it provided just enough light to see the steps leading down to the complete darkness of the sound. Far in the distance the mainland was dotted with tiny lights.

There was something to be said about Long Island during this time of year when everything seemed so still and quiet. If she hadn't been too lazy to get dressed, then put on boots and a coat, Penelope would have wandered around outside despite the freezing temperatures.

As she stared, she thought she saw movement in the shadows down below. Penelope leaned in closer to the windows and sure enough, two figures emerged into the pale light cast by the moon.

Raymond and her own maid, Edith.

"Well, well, well," Penelope muttered to herself. It didn't surprise her that Raymond was a tomcat who had no qualms about getting involved with the help. And she couldn't blame Edith for falling prey to his charms; many a young woman had.

Except these two didn't appear to be caught in some midnight tryst. In fact, it looked as though they were arguing. Or at least, Raymond was arguing. Penelope couldn't hear what was being said but could read his expression clearly enough. He was furious.

Edith, on the other hand, seemed blithely amused. She met his tirade with a mild smile of indifference, only occasionally responding with something that seemed to set him off even more.

Penelope could think of a handful of things that might leave a maid having leverage when it came to a man of Raymond's status. The problem was, she knew enough about Raymond to know that most of those things wouldn't worry him. He would have been the first to brag about having an illicit relationship with a maid. If he'd managed to get her into a delicate condition, Penelope suspected he would have been the sort of cad to deny it. This was especially so now that there was no Aunt Agnes who might have tried to rein him in from his wanton ways.

The only other possibility she could think of was blackmail.

But about what? A man with such a loose moral outlook on life to begin with wouldn't have many scruples that one could hold over his head to threaten him with.

Maybe it had something to do with Agnes's death?

That had Penelope going rigid with alarm. Perhaps she should rethink her opposition to going outside after all. She sprung up from the window seat and rushed to grab her long coat to throw on. After wrapping it tightly around her, she slipped her feet into a comfortable pair of winter shoes.

She tip-toed out of her bedroom and down the stairway. It was only once she was in the grand open foyer area that she realized opening the French doors that led out to the terrace would surely announce her presence to the couple. With a grimace of impatience she detoured to the left, instead going down the halls that led to the side exit. She silently unlocked and opened the door and just as quietly closed it behind her.

This side of the house held the servants' quarters. At least one of them was sure to be up in anticipation of any late-night needs of the guests, and the rest were probably light sleepers. The smaller windows of the smaller rooms were closer together here, and she had no idea whose room was whose, having never dared venture far enough into the staff area to invade their personal quarters. Still, it wouldn't do to start spreading gossip about one of the guests wandering around at all hours of the night in the middle of winter.

Mostly, Penelope didn't want word to trickle back to Edith that she'd been snooping on her conversation—or fight?—with Raymond.

By the time she rounded the massive home and reached the terrace in back, she could see Raymond angrily storming back up the steps toward the house.

"Pineapples!" Penelope whispered to herself, using the harmless expletive she'd cultivated long ago to avoid getting herself into trouble.

Whatever argument they'd had, it was obviously over.

Penelope pressed herself against a wall in the shadows to wait for them both to go back inside.

"Oh stop, Raymond," Edith goaded, in a rather familiar and taunting fashion.

"No," Raymond responded, though he stopped and turned to face her all the same. "And keep your voice down. Do you want to wake everyone?"

"What's the matter? You ashamed of me?" Both Edith's voice and demeanor were kittenish, as though she were flirting. But it only seemed to anger Raymond even more. He stormed back toward her and grabbed her arm, practically shaking her.

Penelope was tempted to intervene before he did something drastic, but Edith just giggled in response.

"This isn't funny. You've gone too far. Tomorrow, I'll be richer than Midas, and then...we're done."

"Are we?" This time Penelope could hear the threatening edge to Edith's voice.

"You got exactly what you wanted out of this, doll. We both knew there was an eventual end to it all, and that date has finally arrived."

"And what if the old lady decided not to leave you a dime?"

"That's none of your concern." Penelope could hear the trickle of doubt in his voice as he responded. Raymond let go of Edith in frustration and stormed back up the stairs.

The moon was now high enough for it to reach the bottom steps where he'd left Edith. Penelope could clearly see her face, which sported a look of pure venom. Despite her earlier taunting and insouciant manner, she was not happy with how the discussion had ended.

Penelope watched Edith slowly ascend the stairs. She almost realized too late that she would probably be returning to her quarters via the side entrance. Instead, Edith boldly followed the same path that Raymond took, through the French doors into the main part of the house. At this time of night she probably figured there would be no one up to discover her.

It worked fine for Penelope, who relaxed now that she was no longer in danger of getting caught. While she waited to be sure they had both returned to their respective beds, she considered everything she had heard.

Obviously Raymond and Edith had some sort of intimate relationship, beyond just a simple dalliance. Still, there was something odd about it. This hadn't seemed like a lover's spat, or even that of a woman scorned. What had Raymond meant when he'd said Edith had "gone too far?"

Having left the side door unlocked, she chose to re-enter the house that way so she could lock it behind her. She paused by the windows in order to hear any indication that Edith had returned to her rooms. All she heard was utter silence.

After what seemed like an eon, the cold eventually had Penelope moving forward again, carefully as it was almost pure darkness on this side of the house. She stumbled over an uneven brick in the walkway and let out a small cry, stopping herself too late. She froze in place, waiting for anyone to notice.

Only one light came on. Penelope once again pressed herself into the side of the house, in case it was Edith. In her periphery she could see the face that peeked through the curtains was that of Arabella. Either she was a light sleeper or she'd already been awake. Penelope hadn't even been that loud. Arabella peered out into the brush beyond the path with a frown. Penelope waited, holding her breath.

"Silly raccoons," she heard the cook mutter before snatching the curtains closed again.

When the light went out once again, Penelope continued on, more carefully and quieter than before. Snooping was slightly more heart-racing than she'd predicted. But there was a certain thrill, mostly because the worst that might happen was that Edith and Raymond would know they'd been spied upon. She removed her shoes once she was back inside with the door closed and locked behind her. From there she padded back up to her bedroom.

Sleep eluded her even more now. She'd snuck outside seeking answers and came back with more questions than before. Namely, what had Edith and Raymond been arguing about?

CHAPTER TWELVE

THE NEXT MORNING, THE DAY THE WILL WAS TO BE read, Penelope chose to have breakfast in her room rather than go downstairs and join the other guests. It was a calculated decision that would give her more than a brief moment with Edith to chat in private.

Penelope pressed the button situated on the nightstand next to her bed to ring for service. While she waited, she rehearsed exactly how she had decided to approach this. She knew that she could turn to Chives to get more details about Edith's prior employment and background. However, certain things could only be gathered by talking to her in person.

"Good morning, Edith," she greeted pleasantly as the maid entered the room. "I trust you had a good night's sleep?"

"Fine, thank you ma'am," Edith replied without batting an eye.

After Pen ordered a light breakfast, she considered Edith with a look of concern. "I was thinking...I'm sure you're probably worried about the state of your employment, being that the owner of the house has recently passed. Who knows which of us will inherit? Most likely Agnes's nephew, Raymond."

Penelope paused ever so briefly to see if that elicited any reaction. Edith masterfully stared back with nothing more than polite interest.

"I'd be happy to offer a reference even after such a short period of knowing you. I'm sympathetic to your plight, having only worked here a week, during which the lady of the house...well, you know."

"That's very kind of you, ma'am."

Penelope was certain she'd seen the briefest flicker of sardonic amusement, but perhaps that was just her imagination. It wouldn't do to start casting aspersions on the poor girl if the only thing she was tangled up in was nothing more than a lover's spat. Perhaps she had played a small prank on Raymond who had simply overreacted last night.

Suddenly, Pen felt bad. She was using her position to pry—or meddle, as Cousin Cordelia would put it. And if Edith had something to hide, she was a master at keeping it well hidden.

"That will be all, Edith. Thank you."

"Yes, ma'am," Edith said, curtseying once again before leaving.

As the time for Mr. Wilcox's arrival neared, the air in the mansion seemed infused with a strange mix of melancholy for the deceased and excitement at the prospect of what the deceased may have left to each of the guests.

Penelope had hoped to meet with Mr. Wilcox before the reading of the will to discuss Agnes's state of mind. As the attorney who had presumably helped her create the will, surely he must have sensed something during their meetings that would indicate whether or not she was anticipating an early death, particularly at her own hands—or perhaps the hands of another. He was also more likely to know her financial situation, considering the fake painting.

It was not to be. When she and Cousin Cordelia left their bedrooms, Major Hallaway and Lottie were leaving their room at the same time.

"Good morning," Penelope said graciously.

"Good morning," the major responded, his eyes narrowed as though he was meeting an enemy on the field of battle. A pointless frame of mind to have, Penelope thought. The will was already written, after all, and Agnes was certainly in no position to change her mind. Besides, he was family. Didn't obligation dictate family would get the lion's share?

At least Lottie was dressed appropriately for the occasion. She was in a black dress that fell demurely down to her ankles. The sailor's collar added an innocent touch that seemed rather incongruous to the woman that sported it.

"Good morning," Penelope offered to her with a subtle smile.

"Good morning," Lottie replied, her chin lifted in a slightly lofty manner.

Suddenly, Penelope wanted this to be over. As she followed them down to the study, she had the distinct feeling of being Daniel led to the lions' den. It was understandable that relatives would be wary of an unrelated interloper such as herself. There was no reason Major Hallaway and his wife would have known how close she was to Agnes.

Then there was Raymond, who expected to get quite a

bit of money if last night's overheard conversation was any indication. Yesterday, he had seemed rather blasé about it all, but Penelope sensed he was hoping to be left a significant amount.

Mrs. Mayweather was the only other odd person out. Even she had known Agnes much longer than Penelope had. It also seemed since becoming a widow, Agnes and she had grown closer. However, she didn't seem to want for much. Her clothes and jewelry, while old-fashioned were of high quality.

Still, money was money, and Agnes had enough of it to turn even those closest to her into...murderers.

Major Hallaway and Lottie took two armchairs near the desk. Penelope led Cousin Cordelia to the couch to the left of them, facing the desk. Since Mr. Wilcox hadn't bothered to arrive early, she wished she hadn't thought of coming down so soon. The reading wasn't due to begin for another thirty minutes.

"I see the early birds are here awaiting their bite of the worm."

Penelope turned to acknowledge Raymond's arrival. He'd had the decency to wear a dark suit as well, though the cut of his was much different from the conservative lines of the major's. He strolled in as carefree as ever, as though nothing had happened last night.

"By noon we could all be millionaires. What do you say we throw a little party if that's the case?"

Cousin Cordelia tutted in dismay.

"Perhaps it would be more fitting to at least wait until *after* Agnes's funeral?" Penelope stated, giving him a censuring look.

"Yes, yes," he said, waving a hand as though that was

nothing more than a simple formality. "Dearly departed and all that jazz."

"Young man, it is quite apparent that the Sterling side of Agnes's family is sorely lacking in anything resembling manners, proper behavior, or common decency. Why it is that my cousin indulged you for so long is beyond me. If it had been left up to me you would have been sent packing as soon as you darkened my doorway."

"Well then, I suppose it's lucky for me I got stuck on the Sterling side of the family," Raymond taunted back with a wink as he fell into an armchair opposite where Major Hallaway and Lottie were sitting.

Penelope wanted to scream in frustration. At this point, she didn't care what the will revealed. In fact, she'd be grateful if Agnes did make them all millionaires. At least it might put an end to this bickering, criticism, entitlement, and taunting.

"I think while I wait, I'll make myself a drink. Might as well start celebrating early," Raymond said, suddenly jumping back up.

Both the major and Cousin Cordelia were appalled. Lottie looked as though she'd like to join Raymond as he left to go to the parlor room. Penelope couldn't deny wanting a drink herself, or perhaps some of her cousin's medicine. Her nerves were being run ragged.

Mrs. Mayweather arrived before Raymond returned. She flashed a quick, self-deprecating smile toward everyone as she took a seat on the couch on the other side of Penelope.

"It somehow feels wrong to be here today. Yes, Agnes and I were close acquaintances, but I feel rather villainous benefiting from her death, especially considering..." She allowed the end of that sentence to hang. No one wanted to mention the word suicide, especially today of all days.

"I suppose we should take comfort in knowing that these were her final wishes, whatever they may be," Penelope said, if only to ease the gravity of Mrs. Mayweather's statement.

"It seems we're all finally here," Raymond's voice sang out from the doorway as he reappeared brandishing a bottle and a glass. "I brought the entire bottle of bourbon just in case. It seemed the most fitting no matter which way the wind blows for us. Who knows? The stingy old bird may have only left us one cent."

This time even Penelope and Lottie joined in casting looks of disapproval his way. Penelope studied him as he fell back into the armchair once again, and suddenly she understood. This was all a facade. His nerves were probably even more frayed than anyone else's. It made her curious once again what that conversation with Edith had really been about. It also made her wonder what his relationship with Agnes was truly like.

At ten on the dot, Mr. Wilcox arrived, led in by Chives. His presence created a sudden buzz in the air that Pen could feel prickling against her skin. Everyone studied him, looking for clues as to what the brief-case he was holding might reveal. In turn, he cast no more than a perfunctory glance at each of the people seated in the study.

"Thank you," he said, dismissing Chives, who dutifully closed the door behind him as he departed.

Mr. Wilcox took his place behind the desk and set his case down. "I'm not one to dilly dally with pleasantries and preliminaries. I have one job to do and that is to impart the wishes of my client, Agnes Sterling. I shall be reading her last will and testament word for word, exactly as written so there is no miscommunication or misunderstanding. Is that clear?"

The silence in the wake of that answered the question for him.

Penelope was thankful for his brusque and sensible manner. After all, there was no reason to draw this out.

"Very good," Mr. Wilcox said as he pulled out the will and held it close enough to read. "'I Agnes Sterling....'"

For all his talk of eliminating any preliminaries there certainly were many to be had in Agnes's will. Or perhaps Penelope, like everyone else, was simply holding her breath in anticipation of the parts that were relevant to her.

"'To my nephew Raymond Colley...'" As though sensing the lull that had overcome his audience, Mr. Wilcox paused long enough to ensure they were now appropriately alert. All he had to do was note how everyone had moved ever so slightly to the edge of their seats. "'You are my beloved sister's only child and as such I've felt a familial obligation to support you. Over the past two years, I've become acutely aware of how resourceful you are at making your own way in life, beyond that of holding a job. Thus, I leave the sum of ten thousand dollars to help you become comfortably situated as you continue in your profitable endeavors.'"

"Wait...what?" Raymond said, sitting up and leaning forward. "Ten thousand dollars? Nothing more?"

Penelope certainly wouldn't have scoffed at that amount, especially after the past three years. It was far more than a comfortable sum for the average person.

Agnes's statement regarding his "profitable endeavors" was peculiar. Penelope had assumed his fancy clothing and expensive accessories had been as a result of Agnes generously doting on him.

"Was the old girl broke, after all?" Raymond shot up from his seat and stalked toward the desk where Mr. Wilcox sat. "Let me see that thing!"

"*Mr. Colley*." Mr. Wilcox's voice was curt but loud enough to stop Raymond in his tracks. "You will return to your seat so I may proceed with the reading of the remainder of the will."

"I won't!" Raymond said, stomping his foot. He sounded and looked so much like a petulant child, Penelope nearly coughed out an unfortunate laugh. As it was, she did feel a bit sorry for him. To have an aunt worth so much leave the equivalent of a pittance must be a painful shock, if only with respect to what that said regarding her feelings toward him. "I'm her nephew! Her own sister's son, she says so right there in the will! I deserve more than anyone here!"

"I'm not here to comment on family matters or Miss Sterling's regard for you," Mr. Wilcox said in a frank voice.

"Perhaps Agnes took issue with the manner in which you choose to go through life. From my vantage point, I've only seen evidence that it consists solely of drinking, philandering, and being disrespectful to others," Mrs. Mayweather commented.

"Damn you!" Raymond snarled, turning on her, he swiveled back to Mr. Wilcox. "I didn't spend the past year cozying up to the old broad just to be left nothing more than ten-thousand dollars."

"And yet, that is what the will states," Mr. Wilcox said in his reserved tone. "Now, I shall continue. If you interrupt again, I will have you removed from the study."

Raymond snatched up the bottle of bourbon. He seemed intent on storming out of the room but thought better of it, his eyes scanning the others in attendance with resentment and suspicion as he fell back down to his chair.

He didn't bother with the glass as he took a long, bitter swig.

Mr. Wilcox shook his papers with importance before he continued. "'To my cousin Major Colin Hallaway, as my only other living relative, I also leave the sum of ten-thousand dollars.'" The room was silent as though waiting for Agnes's words to expound on that, but nothing was forthcoming. It took a moment for both Major Hallaway and his wife to react.

"I beg your pardon? Are you certain you've read that correctly?"

"Hey, now what's the deal? I thought we was gettin' way more than that!"

Mr. Wilcox cast a brief, impassive look their way but made no comment. "Continuing on—"

"You wait just one moment!" Major Hallaway roared, not standing up as Raymond did but certainly sitting up straighter and leaning in toward Mr. Wilcox, filled with vigorous outrage. "I'd like to know what this means! I understand leaving such a comparatively paltry sum to this...ne'er-do-well," he said, flinging an arm toward Raymond, "but I've given her no cause for such an insult!"

"Yeah, we barely even knew the old lady," Lottie protested.

Penelope thought perhaps that answered the question for them but kept that to herself.

"Once again, I'm not here to comment on family matters."

Major Hallaway was sensible enough to remain quiet before he too was met with the threat of removal.

Mr. Wilcox continued. "'To Iris Mayweather, this past year has been enlightening. Reconnecting with someone from my past has been a welcome addition to my life, even one with whom I may not have been the greatest of friends as a girl. But with age comes wisdom and a willingness to let bygones be bygones. While your situation is such that you have no need for my financial assistance, I feel it is fitting for me to convey my gratitude for your companionship. Thus, to Iris Mayweather, I leave the sum of ten-thousand dollars.'"

Mrs. Mayweather stared at Mr. Wilcox for a moment, then exhaled slowly. "I see," she whispered, though Penelope could feel her deflate with disappointment.

Penelope couldn't help thinking it did seem a tad insulting, particularly since that very same amount seemed to have some taint of condemnation when applied to Raymond and Major Hallaway.

"It seems we have a theme here," Raymond said with a lazy, humorless smile as he lifted his bottle toward Mrs. Mayweather.

"'To Penelope Banks—'" Mr. Wilcox continued. By now, Pen had an idea of what was coming. She'd no doubt be getting ten-thousand dollars as well, but she was far more curious as to what Agnes's final comments about her would be. It would be bittersweet, perhaps enough to make her cry, but in a way those words would be far more meaningful to her than the money. However, there was no preamble or sentimental commentary, just one simple end to the sentence: "'—I leave the sum of five million dollars.'"

CHAPTER THIRTEEN

THE STUDY WAS IN AN UPROAR.

Next to Penelope, Cousin Cordelia seemed to have fainted. On her other side, Mrs. Mayweather gasped, then shot Pen a look of such resentment, Penelope flinched at the force of it. At Penelope's reaction, she shamefully averted her gaze and turned away, but her body remained rigid with obvious anger.

Raymond was back out of his seat. "What's this about? I don't care if you kick me out, that amount is absurd, especially in light of what she's left to her own *nephew*."

"I have to agree with him, I'm afraid." Major Hallaway was standing now as well. "I would like to officially announce my intention to contest the will. When was this one written? Surely a woman who ends her own life isn't in the right frame of mind to coherently determine what's to become of her rather significant wealth." He cast a hard, narrow-eyed look toward Penelope. "And who knows what this one has been up to, snaking her way into Agnes's good graces like the serpent in the Garden of Eden. This will not stand!"

"Yeah, we can fight this, can't we, lovey?" Lottie said, scowling at Penelope.

"We can and we will."

"No, you will not. Not unless you want to lose everything." Mr. Wilcox's voice breaking through the noise was enough to silence them. Everyone turned their attention back toward him.

He met each of them with a look so harsh he transformed them into perfect school children, shamed into sitting back down and remaining quiet.

"There is a very clearly stated clause at the end of the will, which I would have eventually gotten to, but I see that need dictates I address it now. Any of Agnes's named beneficiaries who decide to contest this will shall receive nothing, a perfectly legal threat which is her absolute right to include and shall be mercilessly enforced." He leaned in over the desk and for the first time Penelope saw something in the way of emotion in his stony gaze. "Before any of you get it into your heads that you might have a fighting chance, I should remind you that I was the one entrusted with the creation and execution of this will. I've been at this game longer than some of you here have been alive, and I am *very* good at what I do. I guarantee many of the lawyers you might hire to do your bidding would agree. I am not to be trifled with on this matter."

There wasn't much argument to be had in the face of that, which meant the others had no one to turn their anger on except Penelope, who was still recovering from the last part of the will that had been read.

Five million dollars! It was an astronomical sum.

"Does she offer any explanation at all?" Penelope managed to eke out, her words struggling in her throat.

"Not specifically concerning you, Miss Banks.

However, there *is* more to the will, a bequeathment that concerns *all* of you." That seemed to have a calming effect, eroding much of the animosity in the room. "But I will first finish where I left off with regard to your bequeathal, Miss Banks. 'In addition to the above-stated amount, I leave all of my personal effects and any property not otherwise distributed in this will.'"

Compared to the monetary sum, that seemed minuscule, until Penelope mentally ran through the catalog of Agnes's holdings, at least those that she knew of. It was a rather impressive list.

The temperature of the room seemed to rise a few degrees once again, most of it radiating toward Penelope. Cousin Cordelia had recovered enough to reach out and take Penelope's hand, squeezing it in support. Penelope was grateful for the gesture, but the last thing she wanted was any of that resentment targeting her cousin as well.

Thankfully, Mr. Wilcox continued. "'In addition, I am granting tenancy rights at the property located at 1110 Stoneybrook road, in the city of Glen Cove, in Nassau County, of New York State to the following individuals: Raymond Colley, Major Colin Hallway, Iris Mayweather, and Penelope Banks. They and any guests of theirs shall be allowed complete access and residency. Funds shall be made available for a full staff and boarding at the property for one full year starting on the official listed date of my death. At the end of the tenancy, the property shall be donated to the Disabled American Veterans.'"

"What the hell does that mean?" Raymond asked.

"It means Agnes was kind enough to give us a place to stay for the next year," Mrs. Mayweather said in a clipped tone that certainly didn't express any gratitude. In fact, she seemed even more bitter about this than she had about the amount she'd been left.

"Correct," Mr. Wilcox confirmed. "As stated, there shall be a fully maintained staff at your disposal and all meals will be included."

"Oh well, thank you very much, Auntie Agnes," Raymond said, his voice oozing sarcasm. "Does this include her seemingly endless supply of booze or will that tap run dry?"

Mr. Wilcox pursed his lips. "There is no accounting for such an expenditure."

"Of course there isn't. Yet another slap in the face," Raymond said with a harsh laugh.

"So we get to stay here? Rent-free?" Lottie asked.

"Quiet," Major Hallaway hissed. "Our home is in Washington, which hardly makes this convenient."

"Shall I continue, or are there any more questions?" Mr. Wilcox said in a patient voice.

Penelope was too confused by that last gift to even respond. She most certainly did have questions, but none that Mr. Wilcox seemed capable of answering. What did all this mean? What message was Agnes trying to impart with this? Why did she leave Penelope so much and the others so little by comparison?

"To the American Red Cross, I leave—"

"Wait a second," Raymond interrupted, his words beginning to slur. "Let me ask you something, is there anything else in that damn thing that concerns me?"

"As far as receiving anything more from Miss Sterling, no."

"So ten thousand dollars and free room and board at this place out here in the middle of nowhere, huh?"

"If that is how you'd prefer to see it, yes."

"In which case, to hell with this." He rose and stumbled out taking the bottle of bourbon with him.

"I think I too shall take my leave," Mrs. Mayweather said, returning to a more sedate version of herself. She cast a hopeful look toward Mr. Wilcox. "Unless I am mentioned elsewhere in the will?"

"I'm afraid not, ma'am."

She flashed a brief smile and rose to leave, without looking Penelope's way at all.

Frankly, Penelope was glad to see them go. Raymond was a drunken, unpredictable mess and Mrs. Mayweather's silent resentment wore on her nerves.

"I'll be staying right here until every word is read," Major Hallaway said, casting a hard look first toward Penelope then Mr. Wilcox. Next to him, Lottie glared at her with undisguised anger.

Cousin Cordelia remained next to Penelope, squeezing her hand once again for good measure. Penelope turned to give her a smile of appreciation.

"So be it," Mr. Wilcox said in an unconcerned voice.

He continued for what seemed like an hour, listing the gifts to be donated to various charities, organizations, and causes. When Mr. Wilcox got to Agnes's art collection, to be distributed amongst several museums, she spoke up.

"I take it Agnes wasn't aware that at least one of her paintings has been replaced by a fake?"

"I beg your pardon?"

"The Matisse in the parlor room, it's not the original. It's a reproduction."

"What do you care? It's not like you're gettin' it," Lottie said with a frown.

"Though it does raise certain questions. I find it rather interesting that you were the one to initially discover this *supposed* fake." Major Hallaway turned from Penelope to Mr. Wilcox. "Isn't there some law or another that prevents inheriting if the deceased has been the victim of one who is named in the will?"

Mr. Wilcox seemed irritated by this question, his gaze still trained on Penelope with concern about what she had just announced. "Even if there is, it doesn't mean that amount will revert to you, Major Hallaway."

"Yes, but as a relative—"

"I should like to have a look at this painting. Seeing as how the remainder of this will doesn't concern anyone left here," he gave the major a sharp look, "save for the portion about what might happen if the will is contested, I would suggest we break to do that."

When there were no objections, everyone rose to head to the parlor. Penelope could hear the major grumbling under his breath about this being a perfect waste of time as they left.

In the parlor Penelope led Mr. Wilcox to the painting, pointing out the small mouse-or-rat in the corner.

"Are you certain this isn't just an idiosyncrasy of the artist? Adding that little tidbit for the fun of it?" The way his eyes scanned the rest of the canvas seemed to indicate that Mr. Wilcox didn't think it took anything away from the painting.

"I saw the original when it was first hung. This one is different and that addition certainly wasn't there."

"Are you sure? It's so small, I'd have hardly noticed myself."

Penelope didn't want to address her peculiarity that remembered every detail about the original painting. "We could always ask the artist himself. Henri Matisse is still alive."

"Perhaps with your newfound wealth you could hire an expert?" Major Hallaway offered, earning him a look of reproach from Mr. Wilcox.

"This is most definitely a matter for the experts and the authorities. It's unfortunate that we don't have a date for when the original was replaced." His words confirmed that Agnes most likely didn't know about the switched painting. Penelope tried to think back to when she'd last taken more than a passing glance at the artwork, enough to have noticed if it was a fake. Mostly, it sat in all her memories as a part of the background. "And this is the only one you noticed?"

"I only took a cursory glance at the others, but she has so many paintings just in this house alone I didn't think to check them all."

"Yes, yes, either way, it would require a bona fide expert," he muttered. "Still, I shall be checking in with the proper authorities post haste about this. This fraud may not be limited to art."

"And may have been committed by someone currently under this roof as we speak," said Major Hallaway, casting a suspicious glance Penelope's way.

"I've had just about enough of you accusing my cousin of a crime, all without so much as a hint of proof," Cousin Cordelia said, speaking up. "Perhaps you should look inwardly to your own faults as an indication as to why Agnes Sterling didn't see fit to leave you more than she has. You might find yourself in a rather *fragile* glass house."

Penelope turned in surprise at her cousin who had just come to her defense. Cousin Cordelia was usually the epitome of non-confrontational.

"Well...I-er—I just think—"

"I have to agree, you are teetering dangerously close to making slanderous accusations." Mr. Wilcox said, squinting

COLETTE CLARK

one eye at Major Hallaway. "And I should remind you that Miss Banks is now in a position to hire the finest legal counsel to defend her reputation."

Major Hallaway's mouth opened and closed in outrage, making him look like a fish.

"Let's go, lovey," Lottie said, stroking his arm. She cast one sour look in the direction of the three remaining individuals as she led him away.

"I apologize, I'm usually not so..." Cousin Cordelia seemed flustered and slightly breathless, as though her outburst had been quite the ordeal.

"No need to apologize, ma'am. Sadly, such accusations are par for the course in my experience. Money has a way of turning even the most civilized folk into perfect animals." Mr. Wilcox cast a benign smile on Cousin Cordelia. "And rarely have I seen such an impressive defense of another's honor. You do Miss Banks a great service."

"She always has," Penelope said, reaching out to interlock her arm with her cousin's.

"That said, I should point out that the portions of the will that concern you have been read. You and the others will of course be provided with copies. However, I do have a final bit of business to conduct with you Miss Banks, though, at the request of Miss Sterling, it must be done in private."

"Surely my cousin can stay."

"I'm afraid the instruction of Miss Sterling was quite clear."

Penelope was set to argue but Cousin Cordelia spoke up instead. "No, no, dear. You and Mr. Wilcox discuss your business. I'm afraid that I need a respite. This has been quite overwhelming, I must say."

That brought Penelope's mind back around to just how

much Agnes had left her. Even second-hand, it must feel like an overwhelming amount, never mind the accusations being cast Penelope's way.

"Alright then, if you insist," Penelope said, gently squeezing her arm before she left. She turned back to Mr. Wilcox. "You said there was no more to the will with regard to me, so what other business did Agnes have left for me?"

"Let us head back to the privacy of the study," Mr. Wilcox said, leading the way. "It's a letter, one she instructed you to read only in my presence. And before you ask, no I have no idea what the contents are. They are for your eyes only."

CHAPTER FOURTEEN

DESPITE HER CURIOSITY AS TO WHAT AGNES'S LETTER might entail, there was one thing that Penelope was concerned about. She brought it up with Mr. Wilcox before they reached the study again.

"Did Agnes leave nothing to any of her staff? At the very least, Chives? Beth? Arabella? They and others have been with her so long."

He smiled as he walked next to her. "Miss Sterling created a separate trust for most of those in her employ, as well as other friends and acquaintances, to be distributed upon her death. Each of them will be afforded an annuity that should see many of them quite comfortable. She didn't want them caught up in the turmoil that she presumed her will would entail."

"Turmoil indeed."

"Don't you worry about a thing Miss Banks. I meant what I said earlier. The will is ironclad, even as recent as it is."

"As recent? When was this one written?"

"Only this past Tuesday."

"This *Tuesday*?" That was enough of a shock to have Penelope stopping in her steps.

Despite his assurances that the will was ironclad, there was a slight wrinkle in Mr. Wilcox's brow. "Yes, considering the circumstances of her death, it does seem a tad worrisome, particularly since the only clauses that were changed concerned the other three individuals here this weekend. However, even suicide doesn't negate an individual's *compos mentis*. And I will testify to the fact that Agnes was mentally sound when she created this will."

"May I ask what the former will entailed?"

"With regard to you, nothing has changed," he replied, urging her toward the study.

"So she always intended to leave me that much?" Penelope asked, continuing on.

"Over the course of her lifetime, Miss Sterling has changed her will often enough. Having always been her estate attorney, I can say the first was created long before you were born. However, for several years now, you have always been included as a beneficiary. I'd have to check my records to make sure, but I would say that for at least a decade or so the amount left to you has been the same, though the inclusion of her personal effects and property has only been included in the past several years or so."

"I see," she said, pondering this news. Agnes had included her in her will since even before her mother—the woman who was truly closest to her—had died. It made Penelope curious as to how much Agnes would have left her mother if she had lived.

They were nearing the study and her thoughts returned to the letter. "Was that also when this letter was given to you? This Tuesday?"

He cast a sideways glance at her. "Indeed it was. But let's discuss that behind closed doors."

Once they were back inside the study, the doors closed behind them, Penelope sat directly opposite him on the other side of the desk being that it was now only the two of them.

Mr. Wilcox reached into his case and brought out a single, sealed envelope and handed it to Penelope. Her full name was scrawled across the outside in perfect script.

Penelope opened it, revealing several sheets of paper all filled with the same scrolled lettering that would have been elegant enough for formal invitations. She began to read:

My Dearest Penelope,

If you are reading this, it must mean I've finally passed away. It also means you've no doubt learned of the contents of my latest and final will. I'm sure you have many questions, and I shall try to address them here.

First, allow me to convey just how much your companionship with me has meant. I understand your reluctance to take advantage of my generosity since being abandoned by your father and for that I applaud you. Very few young women brought up the way you have, securely swaddled in a blanket of wealth and means, would have had the fortitude to forgo it all for the sake of your honor.

On that note, If you presume I had any misgivings about your methods of procuring an income, well...I think you know me better than that.

Penelope's eyes had begun watering from the first paragraph, and the cough of laughter this sentence elicited was enough to make the tears fall.

Now, on to the business of why I've written you a sepa-

rate letter. I've instructed Mr. Wilcox to ensure your privacy as you read this for good reason. I'm sure it won't bring you much comfort, and I apologize beforehand.

First, I'd like to explain the seemingly exorbitant amount I've left to you. Mostly, it is to express my fondness and admiration for you. I have no doubt that you will be judicious, wise, and perhaps even cunning in how you manage it, which would be my advice if I were still here to guide you. I only wish I were alive to see how you get on in life, unfettered by social convention or financial need. Such a vast amount might be squandered away in the hands of others, but I have an inkling you will do interesting things with it.

The most pressing reason I've written a separate private letter is that I have a request for you. If I have died by any means other than natural causes or by anything that can only be explained away as an act of God, you can be certain that it was none other than murder.

Penelope gasped aloud. Her eyes flashed up to Mr. Wilcox. He was staring at her intently, the undisguised curiosity about the contents of the letter coloring his expression.

"What is it?" Mr. Wilcox pressed, leaning in over the desk in an almost unseemly manner.

"I—" Penelope paused, realizing she should finish the letter before saying anything. Her eyes dropped back down to the papers in her hands and she continued reading, despite the soft sigh of disappointment she heard from Mr. Wilcox.

It wasn't until recently that I felt the coincidences were too many. I could no longer ignore the upsetting possibility that I am, and have been in the past, the victim of foul play. I have always suspected that the accident with my car was more than simple bad luck. The brakes malfunctioned, but I know Leonard to be trustworthy and a more than competent mechanic. Apart from that, the car had only been a year old, too new to be subject to wear and tear. The damage from the collision made it impossible to prove any evidence of tampering and I was resigned to accepting that perhaps it was a simple unfortunate mishap.

Until the weekend prior to writing this letter.

The convergence of the same individuals who had visited me during the time of my accident was upon me once again. This alone would not have raised my suspicions save for the following concerns regarding each of them:

I've long suspected Raymond of being an irresponsible spendthrift who somehow lives well above his means, in particular the means that I provide for him. I'm not sure how he has lately come across so much gratuitous income, but I'm beginning to have my suspicions. He was never one to spend time visiting with me here in Long Island where I made my home since the accident, but over the past several months, his visits have become almost routine and quite regular. I would like to think that he has suddenly discovered a fondness for me, but I am hardly that credulous. It can only mean he intends to curry favor in hopes that I will be more generous with my allowance. However, desperation causes people to resort to drastic means and I shudder to think how far he would go in his greed.

Iris Mayweather has become a rather puzzling acquaintance. We weren't particularly fond of one another as schoolmates. In fact, I'd rather say we had a mutual dislike of each other. Still, I realize the passage of time has a dulling effect on old resentments. There is also something to be said for making amends with old familiar faces as the years pass and there are fewer and fewer of them left.

Still, there is something very strange about it all, her

appearing in Long Island after almost forty years of no contact, particularly as she first arrived only one week prior to my accident. A part of me has suspected she has avaricious aims, though she claims to have been well provided for by her former husband. Still, out of sympathy for her situation, I have been generous with her and assured her that I would leave something to her in my will. In retrospect, perhaps foolish on my part, but I do like to believe the best in people.

Finally, there is my cousin Colin. He has been far less coy about his requests for money, which in its own way is somewhat refreshing. He is family, so I was willing to give him an amount, which I will not reveal here as that is between Colin and myself. His reappearance here was rather surprising, most particular his assertion that I sent a letter inviting him to visit, which I most certainly did not. I attributed his insistence of its existence to some facade to maintain his dignity before he made yet another request for money, which he in fact did. This time I was not so generous. It is quite apparent where his failings are with regard to his finances and I refuse to be an enabler in that regard. I told him as much. I imagine neither the major nor his wife were happy about that.

I realize that the above information does nothing more than perhaps cast mild suspicion on each individual, not nearly enough to even convince a jury of guilt. Frankly, it's the only reason I haven't gone to the police, for fear of seeming like a dotty, paranoid old woman.

However, there is one salient fact that remains: all parties were visiting me around the time of my car accident and all parties are currently staying with or near me as I write this. If you are reading this letter, I fear at least one of them has gone so far as to hasten receiving anything I may have left them in my will, assuming I would be as generous after death as I have been in life.

They are kin or acquaintance, and being that I have no tangible proof of any guilt, I do feel some obligation toward them even after death. It is not in me to be spiteful and miserly, especially as I may have cast innocent parties in an unfavorable and unfair light. As such I have given each a very tidy sum that should see them more than comfortably settled, though they may all be disappointed in the amount.

I have also included a clause in my will that allows all of them to stay at my house in Long Island for a full year. I expect at least some of them will take advantage of this and stay long enough for you to study them in the hopes they may give something away that solidifies their guilt.

If I am wrong, and I hope I am, this will all have been for naught and this letter will be meaningless. In that case, perhaps I have given in to the paranoia that seems to afflict so many when they reach an age where death looms ever closer. If I am right, I can at least rest in peace knowing that I've done what I can to bring justice to myself.

I realize there is not much to go on and the onus I've laid at your feet is quite burdensome. However, I trust you more than anyone, not only with my reputation and legacy but a sense of justice.

I expect you will involve the authorities, if they haven't already been brought in. However, I know you have the intelligence and curiosity to help discover who the culprit is and also the determination to carry on when others may give up. You are the cleverest young woman I know with a mind that works in ways I can barely comprehend. I say that as a compliment, of course. I've always admired the way your special "peculiarity" works, and if anyone can puzzle this one out, it is you Penelope.

With my love, admiration, and appreciation,
Agnes Sterling

When Penelope was done, she lowered the papers to her lap and met Mr. Wilcox with a steady, piercing gaze.

"Agnes was most definitely murdered."

CHAPTER FIFTEEN

PENELOPE STUDIED MR. WILCOX AS HE READ AGNES'S letter. He seemed to be suffering the same mix of emotions that overcame her as she'd read it, though without the sentimentality she felt. When he was done, he set the letter down and stared off to the side in thought for one moment before turning to her.

"This does answer some questions for me. I would have never taken Miss Sterling as one to commit suicide. At least now I understand her insistence on changing the will earlier this week."

"So you suspected murder as well."

"Not so much that, but it was her desire that the will be read as soon as possible after her death. It is rather convenient that all the beneficiaries are here under the same roof."

"It is," Penelope agreed. "Which of them do you think did it?"

"That is something for the police to determine." He gave Penelope a penetrating look, as though predicting she

123

would argue, particularly after having read Agnes's request in her letter.

"The same police who declared her death a suicide in the first place?" Penelope returned.

"The circumstances surrounding her death seem to have warranted it at the time. Trust me, I inquired. Even now, I can't imagine how it could have been anything else." He stroked his white mustache in thought. "Still, this is officially a police matter. Despite Miss Sterling's request, you won't find me condoning any layperson playing the detective. This isn't a Sherlock Holmes novel, young lady, we are dealing with a possible murderer."

Penelope realized it would be pointless to argue with him. Just because he wouldn't support her in her efforts didn't mean she wasn't going to do exactly as Agnes had requested. Even if she hadn't requested it, Penelope's mind couldn't help but go to work reconsidering all the suspects, something Agnes must have predicted would happen.

Mr. Wilcox studied her as though he knew exactly where her head was. "This letter is evidence. I intend to deliver it to the police."

"Of course." Penelope said indifferently. Every word was already etched into her memory. "But I'm going with you."

She wasn't about to let a bunch of flatfooted, obviously inept policemen handle this case and miss certain clues once again.

"I see no reason to hesitate," she hinted.

He met her with a wry smile. "Neither do I."

Leonard drove them to the Glen Cove police station. The city had become independent just after the Great War and, being one of the wealthier parts of Long Island, now had its own police force.

Penelope had decided she would allow Mr. Wilcox to do the talking. He was older and, more importantly, a man, thus, bound to be met with the sort of deference that might get things done.

The policeman sitting at the front desk studied them long enough to realize they might be important people. He sat up a little straighter as they approached, greeting them in a professional manner. "Can I help you?"

"I would like to speak to the individual in charge of the Agnes Sterling case."

Being that her death had only happened a few nights ago, and there probably wasn't much in the way of serious crime in Glen Cove, the officer didn't need to be reminded of which case that was. Still, the confrontation of a man as serious as Mr. Wilcox and the strange addition of a young woman next to him was enough for him to realize that this situation should probably be dealt with by someone higher up the hierarchy than himself.

"Let me get the chief."

That at least instilled a bit of hope in Penelope. After a moment the police chief arrived. He seemed to have an aura of competence and concern which would hopefully translate into him taking this seriously.

"I'm Chief Higgins. I understand you wanted to discuss the Agnes Sterling, er," he cast a quick sidelong glance toward Penelope, "death?"

"Yes, we have information that may be vital to the case. Is there somewhere we can speak privately?"

Again the chief cast a look toward Penelope, whose

expression made it quite clear that she had no intention of sitting out on this meeting. "Follow me."

They both followed him directly to his office and each took a seat opposite the chief behind his desk.

"I am—*was*, Miss Sterling's attorney, David Wilcox. I have here a letter Agnes Sterling placed directly into my hands this past Monday. It was to be delivered to this young lady, Miss Penelope Banks, one of the beneficiaries listed in Miss Sterling's will."

That earned Penelope another look.

"If you read the contents, I believe you'll find that it opens the door to the possibility that her death may not have been a suicide after all."

"More than a possibility," Penelope insisted.

Neither of the other men in the room seemed pleased with her interjection.

The chief turned his attention to the letter. Penelope could already read the skepticism written all over his face before he read the first line. His expression didn't change as he continued. When he was finished, he set the papers down and focused his attention on Mr. Wilcox.

"I can see how this raises some questions. However, I can't deny that the facts and evidence still make a strong case for suicide. She was found in a locked room with no hint of tampering on the door or windows. Further, in her possession, she had the poison and the letter—"

"Did a professional check to make sure the letter was actually in her handwriting?" Penelope interrupted, not caring if it irritated the man or not. "Surely there are experts in that sort of thing?"

Chief Higgins gave her an impatient look. "We checked it against other legitimate examples. Even her own butler was hard-pressed to deny it was hers. This letter has the same handwriting. Speaking of which, this was written on Monday, you say?" He looked at Mr. Wilcox for confirmation. "Who knows what may have happened between then and the night it happened? I've seen a person's state of mind change within a day, happy one moment, sad the next."

He lifted one hand as the two of them began to protest. "I'm not denying your concerns, I'm just pointing out that this doesn't necessarily point to any of these people being a murderer. Mr. Wilcox, as an attorney, surely you understand what reasonable doubt is? This letter does nothing to provide definitive proof. On the other hand, we have the facts and the evidence that my *very competent* detective was faced with when we found the—" His eyes darted toward Penelope before he continued. "Before we found Miss Sterling. I'll refrain from going into more detail out of respect for the young lady present—"

"This young lady knows the details of how Agnes was found, thank you very much. I also knew Miss Sterling quite well, and I can tell you she would have been the last person in the world to kill herself."

Chief Higgins sighed. "I understand that, as a woman, you might be inclined to be more emotional over the death of a loved one, but that hardly—"

"I beg your pardon! My emotional state has nothing to do with—"

"Chief Higgins," Mr. Wilcox interrupted. "At the very least, perhaps another look at the evidence and another round of interrogation might be in order, wouldn't you agree? No one is questioning the competence of your detective or other officers in your department. However, I would hate to have a cloud of doubt or uncertainty cast upon your brand new police department. We wouldn't want any rumors to circulate that perhaps you hadn't done your utmost to ensure a woman's death was adequately investigated? No such rumors would come from myself nor Miss Banks here of course. Still, these things do have a way of getting out."

Penelope held back a smile of satisfaction. Mr. Wilcox was handling this far better than she would have, and in a way that was far more likely to get results. She should have remembered the adage about catching more flies with honey than vinegar. Perhaps the man wasn't as much of a bluenose as she thought he would be.

Chief Higgins cast a sour look at Mr. Wilcox, his mouth tightened with displeasure. "As I stated, I don't intend on letting this lie. *However*, we are a small department with only so many resources. Detective Ames, who was working on this case is currently indisposed, working on another active case. Unless of course you would like me to pull him off that far more urgent matter to handle this issue?"

Penelope could see that he was intent on being obstinate. "Do you have photographs of the scene? Presumably your detective at least made sure that much was done. I'd like to look at them, if I may?"

The chief's eyes narrowed. "If we did, they certainly aren't available to any member of the public who walks in here curious about the case. Now that it seems the case may be re-opened, I have even more reason not to make them public. My apologies, miss." He looked anything but apologetic. In fact, he seemed rather smug.

"Naturally we wouldn't want to compromise this case or any other more urgent police matters," Mr. Wilcox said in a far more gracious tone than she would have used.

"I appreciate that," Chief Higgins said, not at all placated if his expression was any indication. "Was there any other information you had to impart? Some actual evidence, or more clues perhaps?" Penelope could hear the condescension in his voice.

"Ah yes, there is the other matter of a piece of artwork. I hate to overwhelm your force with yet another crime. Still, I think it wise to at least alert you to the fact that a painting of Miss Sterling's has apparently been replaced by a fake."

Penelope hardly thought this was important considering the far more important issue of Agnes's murder. She didn't want Chief Higgins's attention diverted. However, there was a sudden flash of interest in his eyes that roused her curiosity.

"A fake? As in the original was stolen and replaced?"

"Presumably. Though I have no idea when and how. Perhaps something else to inquire about when this Detective Ames re-questions the staff about Agnes's death?"

"Right," the chief said, his expression suddenly clouding again at the reminder. "I'll have to keep this letter as evidence, of course. Detective Ames will be around to make inquiries and have another look at this case when he's available. Thank you for bringing this to my attention. After all, I wouldn't want any aspersions cast on me or my men."

It was a blatant dismissal, and not an amicable one.

Penelope was inclined to stay seated if only to lay a bit of pressure on him, but Mr. Wilcox spoke up first in an almost cheerful manner. "Thank you so much, Chief Higgins. I already feel reassured knowing that you are taking this matter seriously."

He rose from his seat, and a slightly placated Chief Higgins rose as well. Penelope remained in her seat, staring at both of them incredulously.

"Miss Banks, I think we should allow Chief Higgins to get on with his business of the day."

"Yes but—"

"Indeed, I have everything I need and if there are any more questions, I'm sure Detective Ames will get in touch," the chief hinted, making it clear they were done.

Penelope sighed and rose from her seat. She supposed it wouldn't do to antagonize him. He had the letter and had given his word, which was more than she could have hoped for, honestly. All the more reason to abide Agnes's wishes to handle this herself.

"Thank you so much for looking into this, Chief Higgins. Agnes was a dear friend of mine and it's important to me that justice be done." She offered a charming smile, which was met with a humorless stare.

Mr. Wilcox led the way as they left the station. Once outside, Penelope could no longer contain herself.

"Well, he certainly didn't inspire much confidence! I'd think that a letter practically hand-feeding him the fact he has a murderer on his hands would have been enough to—"

"Miss Banks, there is something to be said for diplomacy. A man's pride, particularly that of a man in a position of power, can be a fragile thing, especially when it comes to young women casting doubt on his competence and abilities."

She thought back to Mr. Rademacher, who had been a stark lesson in what Mr. Wilcox was telling her. Then of course there was Clifford Stokes, who, along with her own father, had been the ruin of her, all because she refused to marry him.

"Honestly, I've had enough of men's pride, thank you very much," she snapped. Then, she sighed. "But...you may have a point. However, I fully intend on making sure he follows through on re-investigating this matter."

"As shall I." Mr. Wilcox squinted one eye as he studied

her. "I suppose you also intend on doing your own investigating despite my warning?"

She lifted her chin ever so slightly. "I owe it to Agnes. Don't worry, I don't plan on being *too* clumsy about it."

"It isn't clumsiness I'm worried about. We are talking about murder after all."

"I suppose it wouldn't make you feel any better if I told you I had no intention of getting murdered myself?" Penelope offered a wry smile.

Mr. Wilcox couldn't help but chortle in response. "Just remember, you have five million reasons to live now, young lady."

In all this business, Penelope had completely pushed aside the reminder that she was a bona fide millionaire now. "I'd rather have Agnes," she said quietly.

Mr. Wilcox considered her with a softer look. "Yes, I suppose that's exactly why you were the fortunate one. True affection is worth more than riches. I've lived long enough and seen too much in my profession to ignore that truth."

"How many murders have you experienced?"

"It isn't uncommon. Greed is one of the standard motivators, along with its brethren anger, envy, and pride."

"Hopefully, I won't have to wade through all seven deadly sins to find the culprit," Penelope said with a grin.

CHAPTER SIXTEEN

As the car approached the estate, Penelope stared at the large mansion through the window just as she had yesterday when she first arrived. Today, she viewed it with a different lens. Gone was the nostalgia of over-the-top parties and enjoyable weekend visits with Agnes. Now, it was nothing more than the location where someone currently residing inside was a murderer.

When the car came to a stop and Leonard opened the door for Mr. Wilcox and her, she hesitated before stepping out.

She suddenly felt the weight of Mr. Wilcox's words of warning. Her only reassurance was that, while the suspects knew she was skeptical of Agnes's cause of death, they didn't necessarily know that she suspected one of them. With that in mind, she slid out.

"Miss Banks," Mr. Wilcox said, stopping her before they entered the home. "I feel this little detour has taken us off track from the matter of the will. Technically, everything designated for you in the will is officially yours. There will be certain administrative matters to deal with, changing the title on property, transferring ownership, and of course, giving you access to your funds. I'd like to arrange a more formal meeting with you in my offices as soon as possible. Until then, If you'll give me your banking information, my firm can quickly transfer say, ten thousand dollars today? Will that be enough? It seems to be the theme of the day."

Penelope blinked. Once upon a time that amount meant nothing to her, mostly because, under her father's dominion she never concerned herself with amounts, she simply bought what she wanted. Then after he cut her off, it would have been the equivalent of a godsend. "Y-yes, I think that will be more than enough."

"Good, good. What would be a good day for you to meet with me? The sooner the better."

"It shouldn't be before the funeral," she said as a way to give herself more time here in Long Island to investigate.

Penelope could tell Mr. Wilcox wasn't fooled, but he refrained from any scolding. She liked him more than she thought she would.

"Will the day after do?"

"That will be fine."

"I hope to see you then, Miss Banks." She didn't miss the slight emphasis on the word "hope."

"Will you at least do me the favor of allowing *me* to tell my father about what I've been gifted? I am an adult after all."

"Of course," he replied with a wrinkle of confusion in his brow. "I would never discuss your business with him without your express permission."

"It's just that—well, you left the job of informing me about Agnes's death to him."

The look of confusion deepened. "He insisted on it,

Miss Banks. I simply offered my condolences to him, knowing that Miss Sterling was a friend of his late wife."

"He insisted on telling me himself?" Penelope asked. Now she was the confused one.

"Well yes, I assumed as his daughter that you would have appreciated—"

"My father and I are most definitely not on speaking terms."

"I see," he said slowly. He tilted his head to consider her. "From what I know of Mr. Banks, he seems a rather brusque man, if you'll forgive my frankness."

"Forgiven, if only because I'd use harsher terminology than that," she said with a dry laugh.

He smiled. "It's just that, perhaps he used this as an excuse to simply visit with you. Some people have difficulty reaching out when they'd desperately desire to. I suspect this was his means of extending an olive branch."

"If so, he thoroughly burned it before I had a chance to even accept it," Penelope replied curtly. The manner in which he'd told her about Agnes's death was hardly sympathetic, even if Penelope had needled him somewhat that night.

Mr. Wilcox nodded and exhaled with finality. "Well, I shall keep that in mind, Miss Banks. I will have my secretary call you so we can set up a time to meet. Do you have any more questions or concerns before I take my leave?"

"No, I suppose not," Penelope said.

"Well then, good day, Miss Banks."

"Good day, Mr. Wilcox."

Penelope quickly escaped the frigid cold to go inside. She wasn't prepared to confront anyone just yet. She wanted a moment to organize her thoughts and decide on the best approach. As such, she headed directly to her bedroom and closed the door.

She had just removed her shoes when a light knock came from the door. Knowing it could only be Cousin Cordelia—she imagined anyone else would have had a less delicate touch—she called out for her to enter.

"Penelope, dear," Cousin Cordelia said, hesitantly opening the door. "How are you? Wherever did you disappear off to? I suppose it is quite a bit to take in, isn't it? So... very...much," she said in wonder. "You probably needed some time to yourself, no doubt."

Penelope gave her a weary smile. "Come in, I could use a friendly presence right about now."

Her cousin entered, gently closing the door behind her. "What did Mr. Wilcox want to speak separately with you about? Oh, I suppose you can't say. I just hope it wasn't too upsetting. You look rather drawn, dear."

Penelope debated how much to tell her. On the one hand, it would be nice to have a confidant who knew as much as she did. On the other hand, Cousin Cordelia's delicate constitution would completely deteriorate at the idea of staying under the same roof as a possible murderer.

"It's nothing, I'm fine."

Cousin Cordelia studied her for a moment, then looked away slightly flustered. "Yes, I suppose you have a lot to think over. Your life will be completely different now."

Penelope realized what her cousin was worried about. "Cousin, do you honestly think I'll abandon you? Applesauce! I have no intention of doing any such thing."

Her cousin blushed, which almost made Penelope laugh. She stopped herself in time, considerate of Cousin Cordelia's feelings.

"Money has a way of changing people, dear. Just look

how much you've changed from having to earn it yourself these past three years. I of course say that as a compliment."

Penelope smiled, wondering if she wasn't turning a mild shade of pink herself. She hadn't considered what earning a living and, probably even more applicable, playing cards had done to her as a person. Certainly in some ways, she was far more worldly. It had also definitely made her appreciate the value of money.

Cousin Cordelia fussed with the skirt of her black dress. "I know I'm an old fusspot, a bluenose is what you young folk call it these days, I believe. Young people need to have a bit of fun, perhaps some of it quite wicked. You needn't hide it from me, Penelope."

Her eyes narrowed slightly as she studied Cousin Cordelia. "What do you mean?"

"Oh Penelope, I'm not a *complete* fool. I know you sneak out when you think I'm asleep to go off to one of your jazz clubs or parties or whatnot."

"You know about that?" Her cousin didn't necessarily have the details correct, but even this much was a surprise.

"While I appreciate your thoughtful discretion, you needn't have hidden it from me. I'm not *that* much of a prude."

Penelope laughed. Those nights she'd tip-toed out of their apartment her cousin had been hep to it all along.

"Penelope! What if someone should hear you?" cousin Cordelia scolded.

"Of course," Penelope responded, quickly altering her expression into a more appropriately somber affair. She decided she wouldn't tell her cousin *exactly* what she'd been up to those nights she went out. Both drinking and gambling were illegal, and for all her allowances, Cousin Cordelia was still the old-fashioned sort.

"At any rate, it will be the same as always between us. How dull would my mornings be not having breakfast with you? I couldn't think of living without your company."

Cousin Cordelia smiled self-consciously but still seemed troubled.

"What is it? You're still worried about something, I can tell."

Her cousin pinched at her skirts, her mouth tightening and twisting with doubt.

"Go on, it couldn't possibly be that bad," Penelope encouraged.

"Well...I didn't want to badger you about this right away. I know you need some time to yourself. It can wait."

As if Penelope could let it go after that. "You might as well tell me. One hour or even a day won't make a difference." Frankly, she'd rather dispense with it now, since she planned on being very busy "meddling" for a while.

"It's Mrs. Mayweather."

Penelope felt her body inadvertently go rigid at one of the names from Agnes's letter. Mrs. Mayweather may have seemed the most harmless of all her suspects, but Penelope wasn't going to dismiss her without at least a little bit of investigating.

"What about her?"

Cousin Cordelia's face was creased with concern. "When I left, I ran into her. The poor woman seemed so distraught and, well we spent some time talking."

"Did you?" Penelope could sense where this was going, but waited for her cousin to tell her.

"It's just that, she's been through so much and her situation in life is so precarious and, well, I think it would be the Christian thing to do to at least hear her story for yourself.

I'm not telling you what to do with your money, mind you! However—"

"I think that's a good idea." It occurred to Penelope that this would be a perfect opportunity to find out more about the woman and her motives.

"Really?" Cousin Cordelia seemed so pleasantly startled it was amusing. She clasped her hands together. "Oh Penelope, I knew you had a kind soul!"

Penelope simply smiled. "Shall we go meet with her now?"

"Yes, yes, I'll go and get her. Perhaps back in the study where we will have some privacy?"

"Of course, I'll meet you there." They both left her room at the same time.

Soon after Penelope arrived in the study, she heard a soft knock on the door before it was opened. A smiling Cousin Cordelia was followed by a hesitant Mrs. Mayweather.

Penelope sat in one of the armchairs rather than the couch. The other two women sat across from her in similar chairs.

"First, allow me to apologize for my reaction this morning. I was just so—honestly, I *can't* excuse it," Mrs. Mayweather said, looking perfectly abashed. Her eyes remained downcast, focused on the black silk of the same dress she'd worn to the reading of the will.

"I understand," Penelope said graciously. "It was a shock to us all. I honestly had no idea that Agnes would have been so generous when it came to me. Yes, we were quite close in a way, but that was mostly because of my mother."

"Of course," Mrs. Mayweather said, offering a fleeting

smile of understanding. "After all, Agnes and I were nothing more than former schoolmates."

"Agnes's statement written in the will, it was rather odd no? She made it seem as though you two hadn't been very close in school?"

Mrs. Mayweather stiffened for just a moment, then seemed to sag. Her eyes slowly rolled up from the skirt she'd been focused on to meet Penelope's.

"I suppose I should be honest with you. Heaven knows trying to maintain a facade has hoisted me on my own petard." She breathed out a soft, humorless laugh, then took a deep breath and sat up straighter.

Penelope felt a ripple of something satisfying run through her. It had worked! Her intuition had led to something that might get her closer to the truth. She sat up a bit straighter herself.

"You are right, Agnes and I weren't really close as schoolgirls. We didn't even have the same circle of friends. My parents weren't nearly as wealthy as hers were." Mrs. Mayweather sighed and looked beyond Penelope to the windows that overlooked the grounds of the property. "Agnes was right when she spoke of time allowing bygones to be bygones. The silly spats and rivalries of youth seem trite once you reach a certain age. In fact, the two of us, during our frequent conversations, would laugh about the silly disagreements we had that once seemed so important. To be honest, Miss Banks, it was far more enjoyable reconnecting with Agnes than I initially thought it would be when she first wrote to me."

"I think it was a bit more than silly disagreements, no? You were Letitia, from the stories you told over dinner last night, weren't you?"

Mrs. Mayweather blinked in surprise, not answering for a moment.

"Penelope, that's hardly fair," Cousin Cordelia said, an uncertain look overcoming her face.

Penelope chose to focus on Mrs. Mayweather, whose face had become ashen, before coloring and softening in resignation. "Your cousin was right about you being rather astute." She took a breath before continuing. "Yes, that is correct. I was the one who stole Rebecca's shoes and blamed Agnes. Rebecca had...well her father had caused some financial troubles for my family. It was the mean, impulsive act of a stupid girl who was angry about her situation. I'm not proud of what I did to her, nor for blaming Agnes whom I considered a nemesis at the time. The funny thing is, by the end of that school year Rebecca and I were friends. With Agnes it took several decades. Today, I could laugh about her cutting my hair and she could laugh about getting in trouble with Miss Warren."

That seemed plausible enough. Even Penelope's bitterness at being a perfect pariah among her old friends had thawed long ago and it had only been three years. She briefly wondered what her status would be now that she was practically drowning in kale, but quickly put the thought aside.

This talk of letters made her think of something from Agnes's. Since she was already speaking bluntly she brought it up now. "Did Agnes write to you first?"

Mrs. Mayweather blinked several times before coloring. "I confess I was the one to write to her first. It was, well, it was an act of desperation you see. Though she didn't realize it at the time. Her casual invitation to come and visit with her was a bit of a life boat."

"I take it that your husband didn't leave you quite as much as you may have indicated to Agnes?"

"No, he hasn't."

That caused something to spark in Penelope's mind. When it hit her, she sat up straighter. "Your husband is still alive!"

"I'm sorry?"

"Penelope!" Cousin Cordelia gasped in horror.

"When you spoke of him yesterday, you used the present tense. And just now you did as well."

Mrs. Mayweather went white and her hand came up to her chest in embarrassment.

"That's why you no longer wear a ring. You're divorced, not widowed." Agnes's language in the letter had been ambiguous but now it made sense. When she'd written "former husband" she'd meant divorce not death.

"That's a very offensive accusation to make, Penelope."

Penelope focused on Mrs. Mayweather rather than her cousin, who was positively scandalized. Divorce was a rather touchy subject even in these modern times. Under any other circumstance, Penelope might have approached it more tactfully, but she was too full of energy at the moment.

"No, she's right. Your young cousin has figured out my unfortunate shame. I'm what they refer to as a divorcée." Mrs. Mayweather finally confessed, then became rather animated with anger. "My husband left me and left me practically penniless while he was at it. And to think, *I* was the one to get him into oil in the first place. I saw how popular motor cars were becoming, especially after the war. Airplanes would be next, perhaps even the method in which ships and trains ran, making them much faster. The world was moving into oil. The diesel engine is the future and I had to practically drag him to Texas to make our stake

142

just when the boom was starting. And oh how we thrived, all because of *me* and *my* brilliant ideas and foresight! Then he leaves me for some little—"

She stopped herself before she delved into even more painful territory, but everyone in the room knew where she was headed. It was a tale as old as time, except in this day and age a man could divorce his wife without too much shame, even if it was to replace her with a younger woman.

That at least explained why her clothing was so fine, if a bit dated. Mr. Mayweather had made his fortune and for a while, his wife had benefited from it. Penelope wondered just how long ago her husband had left her. A spark of sympathy ignited in her, having been a woman scorned herself. It was quickly snuffed out by her original mission to find out if Mrs. Mayweather was in fact Agnes's murderer.

"For someone so opposed to modern technology, you're rather astute about advancements in transportation."

"One doesn't have to love the modern age to understand it. As young as you are, I'm sure there are quaint, bygone traditions that you miss. When you reach my age that nostalgia will only grow stronger. I can see perfectly well how technology is advancing. Thus, I can educate myself on a single industry that benefited me—or rather my husband. Still, I do long for the days when things were slower...and certain traditions were upheld."

Penelope couldn't fault her for that. Only yesterday Pen was lamenting the replacement of the bells to call the staff.

Instead, she chose to change direction in the conversation. "So Agnes replied to you when she learned of your plight, writing you a letter of sympathy?"

"This isn't an interrogation Penelope," Cousin Cordelia said.

Mrs. Mayweather was understandably quite wary of

Penelope and her questions and accusations by this point. She considered Penelope's words, no doubt wondering if there would be a trap or another discovery of some secret.

"She did," she replied cautiously. "I thought it was a rather kind gesture. It's one of the reasons I came back home to New York."

"And you've been staying with friends in Oyster Bay?"

By this point Cousin Cordelia had given up, realizing that nothing she said could stop Penelope from prying into Mrs. Mayweather's life.

Mrs. Mayweather hesitated before responding. Looking indignant she eventually answered. "Yes. I stayed with Agnes long enough to reconnect with other friends so that I didn't overstay my welcome with her. I did originally stay with those friends but I could only count on their hospitality for so long. Once the summer season was over, I had to find my own housing. I've taken a room in a modest hotel here in Long Island. That's one of the reasons I came here to dinner so often. Agnes was always generous in offering a room for the night, which helped me extend my finances.

"Perhaps if I hadn't been so intent on maintaining my dignity, pretending that I was still quite well off, Agnes might not have been so...conservative in her gift to me. You have no idea how humiliating it is to be cast aside by a man you helped turn into a success. What it's like to have the world view you with nothing more than pity. How debasing it is to have to turn to a woman you once considered the exact opposite of a friend just to survive. But she was the only one who was kind to me in my time of need so I am grateful to her for that. Even the gift she left me is more than I could have hoped for. After all, I'm not family. It will save me from being a perfect pauper."

Penelope considered Mrs. Mayweather's diamond

earrings, no doubt the same ones supposedly stolen by Julia. If she had truly been in dire straits those would have been the first to go. But Penelope wasn't about to judge her too harshly for not selling everything she owned "just to survive." It was a difficult thing going from a lavish lifestyle to a beggar.

"Now you know all my secrets, Miss Banks. I'm divorced, I have no money, and yes, I may have been somewhat of a bully as a child. All my life, I've allowed my pride to rule me, which has done me no favors thus far. So I'm ceding the reins to humility instead. I realize that you have no reason to favor me with any of your newly acquired wealth, perhaps even more so now that you know this much about me. But if you could see it in your heart to place me in a decently modest home, I could use Agnes's gift to live in some comfort without worry. Yes, I realize that I have tenancy rights here, but as you know, that will be terminated in a year. After that, what is to become of me? I simply ask that you not let a lady of a certain age, one who no longer carries the bloom of youth to attract a husband, die alone and homeless."

Penelope wasn't entirely convinced of her innocence, but she was at least sympathetic to Mrs. Mayweather's plight. She wondered how long the woman would continue with that farce of a name. It must have taken a lot to admit so much about herself, so many things that could leave a woman open to scorn and ridicule.

"I'll see what I can do for you, Mrs. Mayweather," she said for now. It was vague enough to not be a firm promise but it seemed to mollify both women sitting across from her.

"I suppose that's more than I can hope for. Thank you, dear," Mrs. Mayweather said, looking both humiliated and relieved. It sparked another flare of sympathy in Penelope. She realized that if Mrs. Mayweather turned out to be perfectly innocent, she was being unfairly harsh toward the woman.

Still, until Agnes's killer was found, she had very little room for sympathy toward others. For now, she would move on to the next suspect.

CHAPTER SEVENTEEN

PENELOPE DECIDED TO GO FOR ANOTHER WALK TO ponder everything she'd learned today. Once again, the cold had an invigorating appeal that helped clear her head. She headed all the way to the shore to distance herself from the house.

When Penelope made her way to the beach of the next estate's property, she saw a man standing on one of the balconies smoking a cigarette. They caught each other's attention at the same time, and she noticed his head cock to the side in seeming recognition.

"Benny?" she finally called out when she realized who it was.

He waved and disappeared inside, only to reappear outside again, now without the cigarette. He jogged down the shore to meet her wearing a full-length sable coat. Benny was handsome in a somewhat effeminate sort of way with full lips and delicate, patrician features. His dark hair was perfectly slicked back like some film star and his dark eyes glimmered with constant amusement at the world around him.

"If it isn't our own Pen Banks, what a surprise!"

Penelope pursed her lips at the blatant lie. Benjamin Davenport was a relic from her well-heeled past. The only son of a man who owned a good portion of Connecticut, he was what many referred to as a "confirmed bachelor." Such things weren't openly talked about, of course, and his parents were forever wringing their hands with worry that he'd never find a wife and produce an heir, but he certainly made for an amusing acquaintance.

Pen had run into him every now and then at some of the swankier speakeasies in Manhattan. He'd at least had the graciousness to acknowledge her, maybe even chat and buy her a drink. She had always enjoyed being around him with his sharp wit, acid tongue, and more importantly, blunt honesty.

He was also a notorious gossip.

"What in the world are you doing in Long Island this time of year?"

He pouted as though the answer should be obvious. "I heard of dear old Agnes's death. I took advantage of the Hawthornes' mansion to be near you in your time of need."

"Of course you did. You no doubt heard the will was to be read today as well. My, word does travel fast, doesn't it? Whoever your sources are, the *New York Daily News* should be paying them a fortune."

"Don't be like that, Pen. I *had* planned to make my way over at some point to offer my condolences and all."

"I'm sure."

"Okay, yes, I won't lie, the usual tongues are salivating in wonder about just how much kale you ended up with. I was the only one shameless enough to come and find out for myself. Everyone knows Agnes died, and everyone knows you were her pet."

"Was I?"

"You're your mother's daughter. That was enough for her."

"I'd like to think I'm at least somewhat interesting in my own right."

"Oh Pen, you've always been interesting. Now, you're interesting with money. Speaking of which, how deeply are you in the green?"

"Benny, you really are shameless."

"Would you rather I bore you with small talk—or bore you even more with the gossip of the old set?"

Penelope couldn't stop a laugh from escaping. She slapped Benny on the arm. He responded by looping his through hers. She didn't bother resisting. In fact, she figured she might as well take advantage of his nose for gossip.

"Let's walk back, I have something even more interesting than money to discuss with you."

"More interesting than money? Good Lord Pen, these past three years really have done you in. Don't tell me you've gone Amish."

"Don't be silly now, Benny, this is serious. How much do you know about Raymond Colley?"

"Please tell me the old girl didn't leave everything to that scalawag," he exclaimed in animated horror. "The cad does know how to slather on that charm of his, doesn't he? I'm only disappointed his paintbrush seemed to prefer the fairer sex. I would have rather enjoyed a good slathering from that one."

"Gracious, Benny." Penelope had certainly heard her share of colorful language and euphemisms over the past three years. Even that couldn't compare to Benny when he really got going. "But no, she seemed to be of the opinion that he was making his own money elsewhere. You wouldn't happen to know how, would you?"

"Hmm, now I'm left to wonder why it is Pen Banks is so curious about her fellow beneficiary. Did Agnes leave him nothing?" He turned to her with frank curiosity at that possibility.

"She left him ten thousand, now answer my question."

"Ten thousand? My, my, my, that must have been a shock to the poor dear boy."

Penelope could already imagine how the news would trickle back to Manhattan, every young socialite reconsidering their affections. Then again, many of them had their futures so firmly secured they could afford to take on a comparatively penniless "scalawag" or "ne'er-do-well," two terms which more than fit Raymond Colley.

"He attended parties didn't he?"

Benny's lips twisted with wry amusement. "Didn't you notice him at every wealthy home in Long Island this summer? Even those not particularly worth attending."

"I suppose my invitations were misplaced," she reminded him.

"Ah yes, the great shunning of Penelope Banks. I wonder what this next summer will bring?" He arched an eyebrow in a questioning manner.

"Tell me more about Raymond and you might get a clue," she hinted.

Benny laughed. "Yes, the dear boy loves his parties, particularly those thrown by young, single ladies falling above a certain financial net worth."

"Such as say, Claudine Sullivan? Savannah Aldred?" Penelope thought back to Edith's references. Claudine was rather plain and would have happily encouraged a reference after a bit of attention from someone like Raymond.

Savannah was as timid and easily manipulated as a trained pet.

"Among others. Practically had them feeding out of his hand. It's enough to make a boy like me envious. But I do have to give it to him, he knew how to pick them. Only the wealthiest for that one."

"Were any of them particularly generous with him, I mean beyond just an invitation to a party?"

"Oh come now Pen, you know how the game works. No money until marriage, especially for you lot."

It was true. Most young wealthy women were subject to terms that wouldn't allow them to touch any family funds until they either landed a husband or reached a certain age.

So how did Raymond get all this money to which Agnes was referring? If only she hadn't been so cryptic in her letter! Then again, maybe she was as clueless as Penelope.

By now they were back at Agnes's property. Being on the arm of Benny, Penelope felt a little less apprehensive about entering that viper's pit.

"So, are you going to tell me how much she left you?" Benny said as they reached the French doors.

"I still need your brain, specifically the gossip held within."

"Ohh, that sounds ominous. Am I aiding and abetting some nefarious endeavor, dear Pen?" he asked with an excited gleam in his eye.

"No, just..." Penelope sighed. "I'd just like to know more about the people Agnes spent her final days with."

"Whatever for? Worried about being bumped off for your portion of the dough? I do love a delicious squabble, especially over something as tawdry as money."

"Gosh Benny, if I didn't know any better I'd say you'd like to see me bumped off."

"Nonsense, what fun would that be? You're the most fascinating person I've run into this year."

"It's only January."

"Exactly! Now, tell me what this is all about, dove."

"Oh Penelope, you're back!" Penelope turned at the sound of Cousin Cordelia's voice coming from the landing on the second floor. She hurried down the stairs. "I do hope you aren't too cross with me from before. I was only trying to help poor Mrs. Mayweather."

She stopped talking as she approached, casting an appreciative glance at Benny.

"I didn't mean to interrupt you." She gave Penelope a knowing smile.

Pen bit back a laugh at how incorrect her assumptions were.

"This is Benny—Benjamin Davenport. Benny, this is my cousin, Cordelia."

"It's always nice to meet a friend of Penelope's, and such a handsome one at that. How do you do?"

"Positively divine now that I've met someone even more charming and lovely than our Pen here," Benny said. His teasing was perfectly lost on Cousin Cordelia. She tittered like a schoolgirl. "Pen and I were just discussing her newfound wealth. Agnes was such a generous soul, to leave so much to her. What's your opinion on the amount she was given?"

Pen's mouth tightened as she realized how sneaky Benny was being, but there was nothing to be done about it now.

"Heavens, it *was* quite a vast sum, wasn't it? Five million dollars!"

"Well done, Pen," he whispered in awe.

"Benny was just helping me figure something out," Penelope said, moving on.

"Ah yes, our little investigation."

"Investigation?" Cousin Cordelia asked a bewildered look on her face.

"It's nothing," Penelope said, casting a quick glare Benny's way. He simply smirked in response.

"I see," Cousin Cordelia said, looking so disheartened it pained Penelope to see it. She must have assumed Penelope was already cutting her out of her life.

"Really, it's nothing, Cousin, just…silly gossip."

That of course was entirely the wrong word to use with Cousin Cordelia.

"Gossip?" she asked brightening up.

"Yes, of the most vulgar kind," Benny said devilishly. "Money."

"Which is exactly why we should stop right now," Penelope said, choosing the wisest course of action at this point.

"Or perhaps find a more private location?" Benny offered, looking around at the open foyer they were standing in.

"I think that would be best," Cousin Cordelia said, favoring Benny rather than Pen. "Perhaps the study?"

"A fine idea!" Benny said. Since he already had control of Pen's arm he hooked his other arm through Cordelia's and happily led them to the study.

"Now, Miss Cordelia," Benny began, daintily crossing his legs after taking off his coat and sitting down. "How do *you* suppose our Raymond Colley has been making extra money?"

"Wasn't it Agnes who paid his way?"

"The will would indicate otherwise," Penelope reminded her.

"Yes, that is true."

"I would have thought gambling, but he wouldn't be nearly as masterful at it as some people," Benny said, his mouth twisting with delight as he cast a taunting look Penelope's way. She glared back.

"The devil's pastime," Cousin Cordelia said, shaking her head.

"And the sinner's delight. Who knows how many heathens are in our midst?" Benny sang.

"So it wasn't gambling?" Penelope quickly asked, trying to corral the conversation back to its original goal.

"I do know our Raymond currently owes money at shops all over town. The lad does love buying on credit." Benny leaned in closer toward Cousin Cordelia and Penelope held her breath to see what trouble his mouth would cause. "I personally think he was a kept boy."

"Kept?" Cousin Cordelia repeated, her eyes innocently wide with incomprehension. "Whatever do you mean?"

"He's suggesting that an older, wealthy woman was... granting him favors," Penelope explained with a sigh.

"It could have just as easily been an older, wealthy man," Benny offered with an impish smile.

"Oh don't be silly," Cousin Cordelia said, with a small laugh. "What would an older man do with him?"

Benny cast a quick, wry look at Penelope who had to press her lips together to keep from laughing. Benny really was the worst devil.

"If he was being kept, he wouldn't currently be in debt," Penelope said. "His...*friend* would surely have paid off his credit."

"Unless the understanding was over," Benny said.

"Why are we looking at Raymond's finances?" Cousin Cordelia asked with a frown.

Penelope paused to consider the question. In the end, she decided her cousin deserved to know the truth.

"Agnes didn't commit suicide. She was murdered."

"*Murdered*?" Cousin Cordelia exclaimed.

"Murder? Now look what you've done Pen," Benny said with a mocking scowl. "You've officially made me reconsider running back to Manhattan post haste. This is far more interesting."

"I suppose the old set will have to wait to hear the news about my millionaire status?"

"Like a fine wine, it will be so much more enjoyable aged," Benny said, then gave her a shrewd look. "How are you so sure it was murder?"

Penelope decided it wouldn't betray Agnes to reveal the contents of the letter, word for word.

"My dear Pen, I'd nearly forgotten how that memory of yours works. I could have used it a time or two for my own villainous purposes," Benny said.

"So one of the murderers is here? In this very house? *Oh*, I know I should have brought my medicine!" Cousin Cordelia cried. "Perhaps we should leave this to the police, Penelope. I don't like the idea of you involving yourself in this. What if you're next?"

"If I die, the money wouldn't revert to them, they know that. I suppose it would all go to Papa." She pondered that for a moment. "First order of business is to change my will. I think you should get it all, Cousin."

"Oh, Penelope, please don't talk like that," she cried.

"Allow me to be the first to offer my services if you're looking for a kept boy," Benny said, fluttering his eyelashes at her cousin.

"Oh you," Cousin Cordelia said, instantly recovering as she blushed and giggled.

Penelope rolled her eyes. "The point is, none of them have anything to gain from killing me, so I think I'm relatively safe. However, each of them had reason to want Agnes dead for her money."

"Surely you can't suspect Iris?" Cousin Cordelia asked.

"I'm not ruling anyone out."

"And the major? He's a member of the military!"

"And obviously in need of money according to Agnes."

"Perhaps it was that wife of his. *Her* I'd believe."

"Again, everyone is a suspect. But since we have Benny, our fountain of gossip for the young and rebellious set, perhaps we should focus on Raymond while he's here?"

Benny waved a hand in the air. "I served you all the cake I have, Pen, my larders are empty. He likes to shop and go to parties thrown by wealthy, young, available women. Though..." He looked off in thought.

"What is it?"

"He hasn't been gracing us with his presence lately."

"Agnes did indicate he was spending more time here the past few months, no doubt to work his charms even more...just in time for her demise?" Penelope mused.

"That bastard!"

Both Benny and Penelope stared at Cousin Cordelia in surprise.

"Forgive me," she said, perfectly abashed. "I just...he seemed so charming and handsome. To *think*!"

"It's always the charming and handsome ones who break your heart, isn't it dear?" Benny said offering a pout her way.

"Indeed."

"That certainly does point the finger at Raymond." Penelope nibbled her lower lip in thought.

"You don't sound very convinced." Benny studied her with one side of his mouth curled.

"I can't figure how Edith fits into this."

"Edith? Our maid?" Cousin Cordelia was back to looking worried.

Penelope narrated the events she spied last night.

"And the plot gets even more delicious." Benny greedily rubbed his hands together. "Though dabbling with the help is a bit cliché I must say."

"I think it's something more than a simple illicit relationship. Her references came from the Sullivans and the Aldreds. Which means he must have been the one to frame Julia for the theft of Mrs. Mayweather's earrings. He wanted to get her fired and create an opening for Edith." It irked Pen to see so many young women brazenly used, all so Raymond could finagle Edith into a position. "That's an awful lot of trouble to go through just to be able to make a little whoopee in the wee hours."

"So he hired her to kill Agnes then," Benny said with a wave of the hand, as though that were the obvious answer. "Perhaps that's what he meant when he said Edith had gone too far?"

"So he gets Edith hired so *she* can kill Agnes? Why involve another person? I know the man is a scoundrel but is he that much of a coward?"

"This is exactly the sort of question for the police to handle, Penelope," Cousin Cordelia hinted.

"When the police finally deign to come here, then I'll let them handle it. Until then, I owe it to Agnes to follow through on any information I have."

"As usual, I can see I won't be able to talk you out of this. It's the very thing I feared before we came here."

"Wouldn't you want me to investigate if someone had murdered you?"

"Who would want to murder me?" Cousin Cordelia exclaimed in alarm.

"No one, dove, you're far too lovely a presence in this world," Benny said, pouring the syrup on enough to douse her fears. He turned back to Penelope. "So, where is this Edith? I say we twist the screws right now."

"Gracious!"

"He's not being literal, Cousin," Pen said, frowning at Benny.

A knock on the door caused them all to start in surprise.

Chives opened the door. "I apologize for interrupting Miss Banks, but there is a detective—"

"He's here already?" Penelope exclaimed in surprise. She hadn't planned on handing the reins of the investigation over to this Detective Ames so soon. Chief Higgins had implied he might be occupied for quite some time, most likely by design.

"He's in the parlor, Miss Banks."

Penelope stood up and stormed out. This detective was about to get an earful from her.

CHAPTER EIGHTEEN

When Penelope entered the parlor, the detective's back was to her. It was a rather nice looking back. He had a tall, lean build with broad shoulders and an erect stance. His hair was dark, cut and styled in a conservative fashion, which made sense considering his profession. Something about the individual parts made a fairly attractive picture.

She reminded herself that this was the detective who had bungled Agnes's murder. That diminished any favorable ideas she might have about him or his attractive back.

He seemed absorbed with the Juan Gris painting in front of him at the moment. Still, he had no doubt noticed the alcohol lining the bar area behind him.

"If you're hoping to make a bust for illegal alcohol, I regret to inform you that the lady of the house has been murdered. Perhaps you should be focused on that rather than the artwork?"

He didn't so much as twitch in surprise, his back to her as he continued to study the artwork. "What is your opinion on the cubist movement? I myself find it a refreshing addition to modern art. I suppose with the gradual move away from realism over the past fifty or so years, we were bound to end up here. I think in the near future we may find ourselves staring at nothing more than splatters against a canvas and calling it fine art. There's something to be said for being forced to puzzle things out rather than have them presented to you in a frank fashion. Though, many of the old masters weren't without their own cryptic touches, which in a way made for even more of an enigma."

"If you're looking for a mystery, I believe I just mentioned a rather glaring one for you to solve?"

He spun around to face her and the way his eyes fell on her caused something perfectly wicked to ripple through her veins.

Though, perhaps it had more to do with the way her eyes fell on him. He was quite handsome, enough to grace the silver screen or magazines, with dark hair and eyes that had lashes most women would envy. But there was nothing feminine about the angular features of his level brow, bladed nose, and square jaw.

The one detracting feature was the scar that started at the lower part of the right side of his face and ran down his neck. It was a burn mark of some kind that pulled at the skin just below his ear. The scar may have sullied any perfection, but it also made him more interesting to look at. Penelope could barely tear her eyes away from him.

Since the Great War Penelope had seen many such scars, some of them far worse than this. The detective was fortunate that his only affected a small part of his face. Some men were too ashamed to even show themselves in public, so disfigured they were, instead hiding it behind flesh-colored masks. But this detective didn't seem at all ashamed, nor did he seem proud of it. He acted as though it was just a part of him, no different than adding a beard or mustache. Still, she could tell he was scrutinizing her to gauge her reaction. Or perhaps he was scrutinizing her for another reason altogether?

Maybe that was just her wishful thinking.

The last time she had felt this way about a man it hadn't ended so well, and even then it certainly hadn't happened so instantaneously. Her attraction to Clifford took a full week to bloom into full idiocy. That was enough to snuff out any hint of desire in her for this one.

"I hadn't expected you so soon. I suppose your other more *urgent* and *pressing* matters have concluded?"

There was a brief flash of amusement and curiosity in his gaze that she didn't particularly like. It made her think he was going to be the sort to humor and indulge her, patting her on the head like a good little girl as he brusquely dismissed her concerns.

I don't think so, detective.

"I suppose you feel a modicum of guilt at having so irresponsibly dismissed her death as a suicide? Well, now you can make up for it. I trust Chief Higgins gave you all the details, including the letter?"

"The letter?"

Penelope exhaled with exasperation. "*Yes,* the letter! Don't tell me he sent you here without even showing it to you?"

"Perhaps he thought it irrelevant to the case." He considered her in the same manner a teacher might study a pupil who was reciting the wrong chapter in class.

"Irrelevant?" Pen exclaimed, throwing her hands up in disbelief. "I'm sorry, but it would seem your police department is even more incompetent than I thought."

"Is it?" Now he seemed amused again, which made her even angrier.

"*Detective Ames*," Penelope gritted out in a patient tone. "Would you prefer it if I held your hand and guided you through this like a child?"

His lips twitched—Penelope chose to ignore how attractive they were when they did—and he clasped his hands behind his back as he drew nearer to her. "I've never been opposed to handholding but I'd like to think my intelligence and competence have matured beyond that of a child."

"Are you quite certain of that fact?"

"Maybe my, ah, *incompetence* has given me too much hubris?"

"Or too much impertinence. Is this how you handle all your murder cases?"

"Perhaps that's something you should be asking Detective Ames."

Penelope already had her mouth open to express another insult, but the words were caught in her throat. Realizing she had the wrong man, a frown appeared on her face and she rested a hand on one hip as she asked, "Then who the devil are you?"

"Detective Richard Prescott. I'm here about the painting. You mentioned one had been replaced with a fake?"

Penelope blinked as her mind shifted gears to that far less important business. "I see the Glen County police department has their priorities in order," she said with a note of scorn in her voice.

"I wouldn't know, I work out of Manhattan. I've been requisitioned, you might say, to handle this. Apparently taking a handful of art courses at Princeton qualifies me. Speaking of which, perhaps you can show me the particular painting at issue?"

"The Matisse," Penelope said, obstinately crossing her arms.

A slow smile spread his face when he realized she was testing him. Then he spun around and headed directly toward it. "My courses didn't exactly cover modern art but I do have a bit of appreciation all the same." He leaned in closer. "And somewhat of an eye. As far as I know, Henri doesn't have a particular fondness for mice."

He was surprisingly observant. Penelope was also intrigued at how perfectly he used the French pronunciation of the artist's name.

"I think it's a *rat*," Penelope retorted.

He turned to offer her a grin, which both annoyed and tickled her. Reluctantly she walked over to join him in front of the painting. This close to him, she felt distracted by his presence.

"There's more. If you, um, look closer, right here," she said pointing to one of the discrepancies, "this stroke is slightly off."

He turned to her with a creased brow. "How can you tell?"

For some reason the last thing she wanted was to look like some carnival oddity with this detective. "I just—I've seen the original. Also, as you pointed out, the mouse is not one of Matisse's touches. As you can see one of the incorrect strokes is right over it."

"You have a wonderful eye, Miss Banks."

A breath escaped her lips which curved into a hesitant smile despite herself as she stared up at him. "I'm just observant."

Something occurred to her and she frowned. "You operate rather quickly don't you? You came all the way from the city to handle this painting? I suppose that speaks more to the Manhattan department than Glen Cove's."

"I was already here today. This isn't the only home that has been targeted, though it is the first with a mouse—I'm sorry, a rat."

Penelope ignored the quip in favor of this news. "So it wasn't just Agnes who was a victim? There have been other replaced paintings? Here in Glen Cove?"

"All around Long Island, mostly the wealthier areas of course. We believe it began around November of last year. So far about five different homes."

"I suppose that makes sense. The mansions are less likely to be inhabited in the winter."

"Exactly, which is why this choice is odd. My understanding is that Miss Sterling made her residence here over the winter?"

"With the exception of her New Year's party at her apartment in Manhattan, yes. She preferred it here since... since her accident." Just speaking about Agnes made Penelope choke up a bit.

A somber look came over Detective Prescott's face. "I'm very sorry for your loss, Miss Banks."

She swallowed hard and nodded her appreciation.

"Chief Higgins said you don't think her death was a suicide?"

"I *know* it wasn't," she insisted.

"Since I'm here and Detective Ames isn't, perhaps you can give me the details."

She blinked in surprise. "Really?"

"It can't hurt to have another detective take a look, even an incompetent, impertinent one with the maturity of a child."

Penelope laughed despite herself. "I apologize for that, Detective Prescott."

"No harm done. Trust me, Miss Banks, I've suffered far worse insults than yours."

Her gaze inadvertently fell to the scarring near his ear then back again. Something in his eyes hardened, as though the insults that stung most had come to him because of that scar.

"Courtesy of my time in France. It isn't always words that hit the hardest."

"Sorry, I—I just..."

"It's fine. Let's uncover Miss Sterling's murderer shall we?"

"Yes, yes, of course," Penelope said, standing up straighter. "I don't suppose you saw the photos of the crime scene? Chief Higgins wasn't inclined to allow me access. Would they have even taken them in the case of suicide?"

"For someone of Miss Sterling's stature, they most certainly did," he said, looking to the side in grim thought.

"That's a good thing, isn't it? I know if I could see them I could discover something that would indicate murder."

Detective Prescott inhaled looking almost angry right now.

"What is it?"

"I think I may be able to grant you access to those photos, Miss Banks. Though, it may be a bit unconventional."

CHAPTER NINETEEN

DETECTIVE PRESCOTT FOLLOWED PENELOPE BACK INTO the study to retrieve her coat. Cousin Cordelia and Benny were still there, the former being merrily entertained by the latter.

"Well, well, well, at least now I know what's kept you, Pen," Benny said, eyeing the detective with a coy smirk on his face. He stood up and reached out a hand for him to shake. "I'm Benny Davenport and this is her delightful Cousin Cordelia. We're Pen's partners in crime—crime *solving,* that is."

"Benny." Penelope sighed with mild exasperation.

"Detective Prescott," the detective responded, a small smile touching his lips as he shook Benny's hand.

Cousin Cordelia seemed rather taken with him as he took hold of her hand next. "Very nice to meet you, Detective Prescott. It's so reassuring to know that a member of the department is here to take over." She cast a deliberate look toward Peneleope.

"We were just on our way back to the police station," Penelope said to quickly get them on their way.

Outside, Detective Prescott led her to his car and opened the passenger side door for her to get in. When he entered from his side, she felt a current run through her at his proximity.

He started the car and took hold of the steering wheel. Pen took note of his hands, large and well-veined, which meant he probably used them a lot. She briefly flirted with the idea of what they would feel like resting on her waist, or the small of her back...or holding her hand.

A small smile graced her mouth as they drove off.

Instead of heading toward the Glen Cove police station, he turned in the opposite direction.

"Where are we going?"

"To Manhattan."

"What?" She turned to look at him. From her vantage point, she had a much clearer view of his scar. It reached to the lower half and back of his ear and down the back part of his jawline to his neck. She found her heart beating more rapidly rather than seizing with aversion. She wondered what war horrors he'd experienced for this to happen to him. There was something to be said for a bona fide war hero.

"Do you object to sharing a car with me?" he asked, his eyes focused ahead.

"Not at all, I just—how in the world did the photos end up in Manhattan?"

He turned to give her a slight grimace. "Not every man with a badge is the upstanding citizen you'd like him to be."

"Like police detectives who look the other way in a room filled with illegal liquor?" she asked with a teasing smile.

The right side of his mouth hitched up. "I leave that business to the feds. That's their bailiwick."

Penelope wasn't sure if that made him crooked or sensible. Either way, it suited her purposes as far as focusing on Agnes's murder.

"What did you mean just now about some officers not being upstanding citizens?"

He paused before answering. "A selection of the public is...fascinated with real crime. There is a market for photos of crime scenes, particularly of well-known individuals. I'm afraid someone of Miss Sterling's status would qualify."

Penelope gasped in shock. "That's...depraved."

"It is."

"And policemen, they're involved?"

Detective Prescott remained silent as the question answered itself, but Penelope noted how his jaw hardened in response, the stretched skin rippling as the muscles underneath tightened. She was no less irate than he seemed to be. The thought of photos documenting Agnes's death being passed around and sold to indulge some macabre fascination was just so...undignified. It was enough to bring her to tears.

"You mentioned a letter?"

"What?"

"A letter, something that made you certain Miss Sterling was murdered."

"Oh, um, yes," she said, sniffing and snapping out of her thoughts. It occurred to her that perhaps the detective was keeping her from wallowing in ideas about Agnes and the photos. "I remember it word for word."

"Is that so?" He sounded understandably skeptical.

For some reason Penelope was no longer concerned about how he might view her peculiarity. She recited the letter exactly as it was written. When she was done he turned to stare at her in wonder.

"Did you memorize all of that?"

"In a way," she said with a shrug. "I—I have this ability to remember everything I see; as though it were a photograph."

His mouth turned down in thought. "That would explain the painting."

"Thank you for taking time away from your case for this detour. Is your department going to be upset with you?"

Once again he paused. "I'm not entirely sure the two cases are unrelated."

"What?" She was beginning to feel like a puppet who could only recite one word, but the surprises were unraveling too quickly for her to keep up. "How do you think they are connected?"

"At this point it's nothing more than a hunch. Since I have you here, do you know how long Miss Sterling stayed in her Manhattan apartment around the time of her New Year's party?"

"I went to visit her when she first came into town. That was a few days before the party. She often left all the details to Chives. He would know for sure when she returned to Glen Cove, but I doubt she stayed more than a few days after that. She preferred Long Island, especially after her accident. What does that have to do with anything?"

"As you pointed out, the homes that were targeted have been vacant during the period of the theft and replacement. Limited staff, if any. In some cases nothing more than a winter caretaker who lived off-premises."

"Whereas Agnes has been residing in her home this entire time, at least for the most part."

"So it would be fairly risky to target her—unless of course one already had unfettered access."

"So you think it was someone living with her? Or at the

very least visiting her often enough to be able to replace the painting without fear of being discovered."

"Exactly."

"Zounds!"

"Zounds indeed," the detective said in a droll voice.

Penelope laughed and slapped him on the arm.

"Careful young lady, I wouldn't want to have to arrest you for assaulting a police officer," he said gravely, though she could hear the hint of amusement in his voice.

"My apologies, detective," she said primly. Penelope turned to smile toward the window, realizing she was enjoying herself for the first time since she'd heard of Agnes's death. That thought put a sudden damper on her temporary good humor.

"Do you think the same person involved in this painting business killed her? Maybe Agnes found out what he—or she, I suppose—has been doing?"

"It's a possibility. I don't want to rule anything out, but at the same time I don't want to make assumptions."

"Still, it is quite the coincidence, isn't it?"

"It is." He cast a sideways look at her. "Is there anything you can tell me about the current occupants?"

"Only Mrs. Mayweather and Raymond Colley would be suspect. As far as I know Major Hallaway and his wife live in Washington D.C. That's it as far as guests, but—" she sat up straighter. "Something suspect is going on with Edith, the maid, and Raymond."

Penelope told him what she'd overheard last night, which seemed like a lifetime ago. She also added what little she'd learned from Benny about Raymond, including the manner in which he had conveniently gotten Julia fired and planted Edith as a maid in the house.

"It's a bit vague, but still suspicious," he agreed, his brow creasing in deep thought.

"But certainly you'll interview her, right?"

"Of course. I plan on talking to everyone who regularly visited or inhabited the house."

"Does that include me?"

Detective Prescott gave her a sidelong glance and smiled.

"*I'm* a suspect?"

"What kind of detective would I be if I didn't suspect you?"

"You could at least be the kind who doesn't resort to trickery. Is this car ride simply an excuse for an interrogation?"

"No, I *am* taking you to see the photographs."

"It's just a coincidence that I happen to fit the profile of your case. Maybe you can use something I've said to pin the crime on me?"

"I don't pin crimes on people, Miss Banks," he said in a serious voice. "And trust me, I won't arrest you unless I'm sure you're the guilty party."

"Oh well, thank you very much, Detective, I feel so relieved."

"You should. Not every detective is as thorough and honest as I am."

"Well, I hope you're prepared for disappointment. I fully intend to exercise my right not to incriminate myself by staying silent." Penelope folded her arms over her chest and stared ahead.

"That is a disappointment, I like the sound of your voice."

No, she wasn't about to be corrupted by his charm. It was an outrage!

"Does it even matter that without me, you would have never even known about Agnes's fake painting?"

The smile that came to his face had her wishing she'd remained silent. "If it helps, you aren't my first suspect. It would really help if, instead of remaining silent, you told me what else you knew about the others in the house."

She didn't take that bait.

Detective Prescott began to whistle. Penelope turned to him with a scowl, which only put another smile on his face. Realizing it would only aggravate her to look at him she turned back ahead.

Penelope wanted to kick herself. This was the second time in less than a week that some man had lured her into a car only to give her bad news, then try to get something from her. She'd just have to keep her wits about her with this one in particular. Detective Prescott certainly wasn't stupid and was probably as cunning as Tommy Callahan.

She managed to remain silent during the entire car ride to Manhattan. When they crossed the Queensboro Bridge her interest shifted away from being annoyed with Detective Prescott to the photograph of Agnes's suite he'd promised to deliver.

"It isn't too far now."

Penelope only offered an audible exhale conveying her indifference.

"I only say that because you seem rather antsy."

"I'm nothing of the sort."

"Hmm, I guess my detective senses aren't quite what I thought they were."

Penelope coughed out a sharp laugh. "Perhaps you're mistaking my being antsy with a strong desire to be rid of present company."

"Well, as I said, it won't be long now," he said in a

cheerful tone.

Penelope wisely stayed silent until he slowed down, bringing the car to a stop in front of an industrial-looking apartment building north of Houston street.

"Here? This looks like a residential building."

"It is," Detective Prescott said, parking. He turned to her with a serious look on his face. "I'll do the talking."

She wanted to argue mostly because she had become so used to being contrarian with him, but she had no idea what was happening. At least until she knew what this was about, she *would* let him do the talking. If it meant getting access to those photos, then it would be worth it.

The front door was propped open and Detective Prescott led the way in. He did have a nice back. She couldn't help thinking, in a moment of stubbornness, that she'd be glad to see it for good as he finally walked out of her life. But yes, it was rather nice.

He led her up to the third floor, then down a hallway. Coming to a stop in front of one door, he banged his fist against it.

Penelope waited, wondering how the photos had ended up in the hands of whoever was on the other side of that door.

"Yeah?" It was a man's voice filled with suspicion and irritation.

"Are you interested or not?" Detective Prescott loudly inquired.

What did that mean?

There was silence on the heels of that, during which Penelope wondered if the man would respond. He opened the door to just a crack to scrutinize them both. He looked exactly like the sort of sleazy individual who would deal in the kind of wares they were after. Then again, Penelope was biased. Still, the oily hair that fell into his face, the shirt with too many buttons undone, the thin pencil-mustache, a trend she had never taken a liking to, and the beady eyes that studied her in particular with a little too much interest made her shiver with disgust.

"Freddy Manchin," Detective Prescott announced in a deceptively cordial voice.

"Is this the proposition you was talkin' about?" Freddy asked, jerking his chin toward Penelope with a salacious grin on his face.

"You'd do best to keep your eyes on me, Freddy," Detective Prescott said just before pushing right past him to enter the apartment.

"Hey now! Who the hell are you? And who's the broad?"

"Now, now, that's no way to greet company."

"You wanna tell me what you're doing here? You indicated you had something for me."

Detective Prescott turned to face him, his expression brightening. "Ah yes, the proposition." He pulled out his badge. "Those photos you purchased of Agnes Sterling? The police weren't quite done with them yet."

Penelope watched from the safety of the hallway as a guarded look came over his face. "I don't know what you're talking about."

"Now, now, Freddy, don't be like that." The detective's voice wasn't so congenial anymore. "I'd hate to have your, ah, privileges revoked from now on."

"Hey now, that ain't right. I run a legitimate business fair and square."

"*Legitimate business?*" Penelope couldn't hold her tongue any longer. "You call selling photos of people who...who—"

"Yeah, and I make a pretty good living doin' it too. Throw stones all you want, lady, but if no one was buyin' I wouldn't be in busi—"

"Hey, I'm the one you're dealing with, Freddy," Detective Prescott said, harshly enough to draw Freddy's attention again.

"Yeah, well I *ain't* dealing," he retorted. "Now, get out."

Detective Prescott came in closer to the man. He towered over him by a good half a foot and had a much sturdier build. The way his expression hardened was enough to have Freddy swallowing with concern. "I'm fully at my discretion to confiscate every photo you have here, Freddy, and then slap a pair of cuffs on you."

"I don't have it, I told ya," he whined.

"How much for them?" Penelope interjected.

Both men turned to face her with similar looks of confusion.

"That's what you do right? In your *legitimate* business, you sell photos? So, how much for the ones of Agnes Sterling?"

"Miss Banks, you're only encouraging him."

"She sure is, and yeah, sweetheart, I'm selling," Freddy said with a grin.

"That's Miss Banks, to you," Detective Prescott said, giving him a slap on the cheek. He then turned to Penelope. "We're not buying the photos. They're evidence. We're confiscating them."

"He'll just keep denying he has them. It's easier this way. Money will get us what we want, and as of this morning I'm a millionaire so I can afford it."

"Hey, a million will do it, lady!"

Both Penelope and Detective Prescott responded at the same time.

"Don't be absurd."

"You're dealing with me, not her, Freddy."

"I'd settle for half a that," he said with a chuckle.

"Oh, hush."

"Again, me, not her."

"How much have you got on you Detective Prescott?" Penelope asked him.

He gave her an incredulous look.

"I didn't get a chance to grab my purse before we left. I can pay you back if it's a matter of—"

"It's not that. We're *not* paying for these photos."

"Oh yes we are."

"No, we aren't."

"Let the dame—er, Miss Banks speak, detective."

"Hush!"

"Shut it, Freddy."

"I can pay you back as soon as tomorrow. Mr. Wilcox is depositing ten thousand dollars into my account today. I think that should cover it, don't you?"

"I'd settle for ten grand," Freddy said with a chuckle.

"Care to tell him where you store your family jewels as well?" Detective Prescott said in exasperation.

"Hey, I'm no thief!"

"Don't you ever hush?"

"Again, shut it, Freddy."

"Detective Prescott, it's quite obvious that the quickest way to see these photos is by paying the man. Frankly, I'd rather have ownership of them—including any film, negative, or slides—than whatever degenerate individual would otherwise buy them."

"The lady does make some sense, detective."

This time both Detective Prescott and Penelope replied in the same manner: "Shut up!"

Freddy pouted, but he did shut up.

"He's right, I am making some sense. Let's just end this."

Detective Prescott sighed. "I've got only about five dollars on me."

"That's all?" Penelope said, disappointed.

"No sale!" Freddy said.

"Shut up!" they said in unison again.

"Pardon me, Miss Banks, not all of us have just inherited a fortune."

"I should have grabbed my purse. I at least had more than that on me."

"I'm sure," Detective Prescott said. His mouth tightened and his expression darkened for some reason. "But no, I'm not giving you money just to hand over to this guy."

"Pineapples!" Penelope hissed in impatience and frustration.

Both Detective Prescott and Freddy couldn't help the amused looks that came to their faces.

"Would you rather I cursed?"

"If that's all you got, I got no photo," Freddy said with a satisfied look.

"How much to just look at the photo? Surely five dollars is enough?"

Freddy seemed to mull that over.

"Make it three," Detective Prescott said in a gruff tone. He pulled out his wallet and snatched out three dollars and shoved them Freddy's way.

Freddy made a show of considering it, but eventually snatched the money and slid along the wall away from Detective Prescott.

Detective Prescott gave Penelope a disgruntled look. Penelope responded with a pert smile.

"Okay, I got three photos of one Agnes Sterling," Freddy announced in such a proud way Penelope had a rare moment of pure rage, enough to want to slap him.

Instead, she snatched the photos out of his hand.

"Hey, you said you'd just look, not—"

One censuring look from Detective Prescott had Freddy shutting up.

Penelope was too consumed with what she was looking at. The photos were much worse than she thought. The camera caught Agnes in bed and she had not gone peacefully. It also fit with what Chives and Beth had told her. The bottle of poison seemed to have fallen from her dead, limp hand and the letter was unfolded right there on the bed next to her. Her Agatha Christie paperback was open face down on the covers. Next to her on the nightstand was the glass from which she had drunk the poison along with a mostly empty bottle of Chanel No. 5. The drawer to the nightstand was fully open.

"I've seen enough," she said, turning her head and shoving the photos away. Detective Prescott gently took hold of them before Freddy could grab them back.

"Thanks for this Freddy. Consider that three dollars payment."

"Hey now—"

"No," Penelope said, grabbing the photos and walking back in to confront Freddy. "I want you to hold onto whatever film or copies of this you have. I'll pay double whatever your usual—"

"Miss Banks!"

"Double whatever your usual rate is," Penelope continued handing him the photos. She turned to Detective Prescott. "What do you suppose that would be detective?"

He sighed, realizing she wasn't going to give up on this.

COLETTE CLARK

"No more than...twenty."

"Thirty!" Freddy corrected. "And this is a special case so—"

"Don't start getting ideas, Freddy."

"I gotta charge what the market—"

"One hundred dollars. Will that do?" Penelope said, glaring at Freddy. "For all photos *and* the film or slides."

"That'll do," he said with a grin that would have put the Cheshire Cat's to shame.

"One week. Hold them for me that long and the money is yours."

"You got a deal, lady—pardon me, *Miss* Banks."

"If I find out that you've sold, or even shown them to anyone else, I will use every single cent of the *well* over a million dollars I have to destroy you."

Something in her voice or expression, maybe both, had him silently nodding and backing away from her.

"You got it, lady."

Penelope spun away, not wanting to look at his slimy face one more minute.

Detective Prescott cast one more hard look his way before leading Penelope back out. Once the door was closed behind them he paused to give her a concerned look.

"Are you alright?"

"Not really," Penelope said, looking away.

He gave her a moment to compose herself. Penelope took a full minute, during which the photograph as vivid in her mind as if it was right in front of her.

"Did you at least notice something that might help?" he finally asked.

Penelope straightened up and looked at him. "Yes, I'm pretty sure I know exactly what's wrong in that photo. But I need to make one more stop before I can tell you."

CHAPTER TWENTY

"WHERE ARE WE HEADED?" NOW IT WAS DETECTIVE Prescott's turn to ask this question once he and Penelope were back in his car.

"Uptown to a place called the Peacock Club."

"I'm familiar with it," he said with a sardonic expression as he started the engine. "Care to tell me what it was you saw in the photos that has me driving so far?"

"The bottle of perfume on the bed next to her."

Yesterday Penelope had seen the mostly empty bottle of Chanel No. 5 placed among the perfumes on the tray near the door to Agnes's suite. The maid who'd cleaned it probably thought it was actually perfume and put it back in its place. Detective Ames probably thought the same when he'd first arrived on the scene. With the bottle of poison right there on the bed next to Agnes, even Beth and Chives probably thought that's where the poison had come from instead of the perfume bottle.

"Is that unusual, a woman wearing perfume?"

Penelope looked at him with a subtle smile. "Do you have a lady friend, detective?"

Something flashed in his eyes, fierce and hard, then he blinked and turned to consider her with a questioning look. "Why do you ask?"

"Don't worry, I'm not trying to seduce you."

His mouth hitched up on one side, the side with the burn mark. It made Penelope think that, under any other circumstance, she wouldn't mind seducing him.

"A woman only wears perfume in bed if she has, *ahem*, company. In Agnes's case, I can assure you there would be no perfume, and not because of her condition. I seriously doubt she would have let that stop her." Penelope exhaled a bittersweet laugh at the life that was lost.

Detective Prescott cleared his throat.

"Are you blushing, detective?" Penelope couldn't help but feel slightly tickled at the idea.

"I don't blush," he said, looking at her with a frown, making him look even more handsome. He raised one eyebrow. "Aren't we supposed to be solving a murder?"

"Yes, we are. And I've just pointed out where the poison came from. That bottle next to her on the bed certainly didn't hold perfume. It was…"

Detective Prescott smiled knowingly. "It isn't an uncommon method of conveying liquor."

"So I've heard." She wasn't about to get Chives in trouble by mentioning that he'd been the one to deliver the "special blend" to Agnes. If this trip uptown confirmed her suspicions, she'd have proof that's where the poison came from. At least she hoped so.

"Then how do you explain the bottle of poison near her hand?" Detective Prescott asked. "She obviously held it at one point."

Penelope nibbled on her bottom lip in thought. After a moment she gave up with a sigh. "Perhaps someone broke in after she was dead and planted it there? But then how would they have locked the door again? Her key was in the room, and both Chives and Beth swear theirs were with them."

"You don't suspect them?"

"Not at all," Penelope said firmly. "They are the definition of loyal. I've known both of them most of my life, and I know how much Agnes trusted and relied on them."

"Which gets us back to skeptics saying she added the poison to the drink herself. There's still the letter, which was in her handwriting, correct?"

"Yes," Penelope said with another sigh of disappointment as she reviewed the photo in her head. Something was there, staring right at her, she knew it.

"We can check for fingerprints, but anyone clever enough to pull this off wouldn't be dumb enough to leave their own prints."

"Yes, yes," Penelope muttered, still trying to figure out what was nagging at her.

"I should say, you'll be happy to know that Chief Higgins said he had enough to reopen the case and—"

"Open!" Penelope said sitting up straighter. "That's it, that's what's wrong with the letter!"

"What about it?"

"It was opened. I should have taken note when Chives first said it was unfolded. Even staring right at it, I didn't catch on right away."

"Miss Banks, perhaps you'll help me out here, after all, I've only been a detective for three years now."

"The letter was folded, or rather, *un*folded."

It took him a moment to understand "Huh."

"Exactly. Why would she fold it in the first place? Only to unfold it again? For what reason?"

"Maybe there was an envelope?"

"Where? Surely the police would have found it if there was one. More importantly, why put it in an envelope in the first place?" Penelope said in an excited tone. This was finally some tangible proof, at least in her mind, that this was no suicide.

Detective Prescott seemed to be mulling it over in his head. "You do make a good point. If she intended to put it in an envelope, she would have done so before taking the poison."

"Which she didn't," Penelope reminded him.

"There's just one problem."

"What?"

"How do you explain it being right there on the bed next to her if she didn't write it? And there's still the bottle that clearly states that it's poison."

"It does, doesn't it?" Penelope acknowledged, her brow wrinkling. "Isn't that odd, don't you think? Why would the bottle advertise that it's poison? That seems like the kind of thing you'd see in a comic."

"Perhaps the murderer wanted to make it clear she was poisoned. But how do you explain it being in her hand... alongside the letter."

Penelope sagged in her seat.

"I don't know but," she gave him a pleading look, "doesn't this all at least seem strange to you now?"

"Strange yes, but not definitive. And we still haven't established *who* the killer is."

Despite herself, a smile came to her face. "We?"

"Well, I do have to drive you back eventually. Until we get there, I suppose we can work this out...together." He offered an indulgent smile.

"Should I be wary of another ruse? I suppose giving you

helpful information *once again* points the finger at me, this time as a suspect in Agnes's murder?"

The smile disappeared and he turned to study her, his face unreadable. "No, I'm certain you didn't kill Miss Sterling."

"Well that's reassuring. What miracle has finally erased the taint of suspicion?"

There was a brief silence before he answered. "I have it on good authority you weren't in Long Island at the time of her death."

"Oh?" she asked, giving him a coy look. It took her a moment to remember where she was the night Agnes died. "Oh."

"Oh," he replied, one eyebrow raised.

"So what, have you been following me? You think I'm involved with…" she stopped before incriminating herself. Her eyes narrowed as she turned to him. "What exactly *do* you think?"

"What exactly *should* I think?"

Gambling. Drinking. Associating with well-known criminals, enough to get a ride home from them. Zounds, the list was certainly incriminating. No wonder Detective Prescott gave her an odd look when she mentioned having more than three dollars. He probably knew she was a gambler. Maybe he even knew she had a reputation for winning big.

"I'm not doing your detective work for you, but I will say this, whatever I may or may not have done, it was out of necessity. It's too bad I'm a woman, I could have made a living being a detective, and a better one than you," she snapped, realizing how immature she sounded.

"I agree." The smile on his face was amused, and Penelope wasn't sure if he was teasing her or agreeing with her. Frankly, she didn't care either way.

"Ohh!" she exclaimed in frustration before turning around and facing out the window.

"If it makes you feel better, I only know because I called to find out about you before I came to Miss Sterling's house. I don't care how you spend your evenings or...who you spend them with. Now that you're a millionaire—minus a hundred dollars, of course—perhaps you'll be more judicious with how you spend your evenings in the future, and who you associate with. I'd hate to see you get caught up in a raid one day."

"I already have a father who is perfectly scandalized by me, thank you very much."

To her surprise he laughed. "I'm sure you do."

Despite herself, Penelope bit back a grin. She thawed a few degrees, enough to transfer her energy from anger to concern as she faced him again. "Am I in trouble?"

Detective Prescott's face softened. "You definitely aren't a major target, if that makes you feel better. The police keep tabs on certain people. You just seem to have a bad habit of being around with those people, for quite a few years now it seems. At least according to what I've been told. As far as I'm concerned, my only interest is in the painting."

"In which I suppose I'm still a suspect."

"Yes."

She had said it almost teasingly, but she realized he was serious. *"What?"*

"I may not be as good a detective as you, Miss Banks, but I'm no slouch," he turned to her and grinned, "or a pushover."

She glared at him. "I think it's about time for me to exercise my right to silence again."

186

"Again, a shame. I think I like your voice even more now."

Penelope chose to ignore that and wisely shut up until they got to the Peacock Club. She used the time to think about the clues she had.

If what she suspected was true about the bottle of perfume, she would not only know how the poison was dealt, she'd have a better idea of who had planted it.

CHAPTER TWENTY-ONE

Once at the Peacock Club, Penelope was over her irritation with Detective Prescott, who had taken to whistling again during the car ride. It was nearing evening by the time he parked in front.

"This time you'll have to let me do the talking. Or better yet, stay in the car."

He slid his eyes to the front doors, which were closed and looked perfectly harmless this early before they opened for business.

"Fine."

Penelope smiled and got out. It was well before opening time, but Penelope knew there were people inside. Lulu practiced her songs during these hours.

She pounded on the door until it was opened by a large, tough-looking man. He peered out with a scowl. "We ain't open yet."

"I'm here to see Lucille Simmons, she's expecting me— Penelope Banks." A tiny lie, but one which Lulu should play along with.

He studied her, then cast his eyes to the man in the car

behind her. Even to people who didn't have regular interactions with the police it was quite obvious what he was.

"I don't think so, sweetheart."

"He's staying in the car."

"And you're staying out here."

He made a move to close the door in her face but she spoke up before he could.

"Or...he could come back with a few of his friends and raid the place."

That was met with a menacing scowl. If Penelope was in trouble with various underworld types before, she had just put a definite target on her back. But that didn't matter right now.

Without responding, he closed the door and disappeared for several minutes. When he opened it again, he grunted something and jerked his head inside, opening the door just enough to let her in.

Lulu sat on the edge of the stage sipping a cocktail. She met Penelope with an arched eyebrow and a wry smile.

"It's not enough to be banned from every card game in town, you now want to get yourself excluded from every club? What's with the copper?"

"A necessary nuisance I'm dealing with that has nothing to do with why I'm here."

"Why are you here?"

"Barney McClintock." Lulu had been her contact for years now when it came to procuring Cousin Cordelia's medicine. She knew every major bootlegging outfit in the general New York area.

Lulu calmly sipped her cocktail, eyeing Pen over the rim as she considered that. "What about him?"

"He sends special deliveries to his favorite clientele, right?"

"You sure this has nothing to do with the heat outside?"

"Surely you know me better than that by now."

Lulu scrutinized her, then smiled. "Okay. Yes, he does. Why do you ask?"

"He uses unusual containers, right?"

She nodded, taking another sip.

"How likely would it be that he'd use a bottle of Chanel?"

Lulu laughed, nearly spitting out her drink. "French perfume? I doubt Barney even knows where France is. And the closest that man has ever gotten to smelling good is when he spills food on his shirt. His guys pay kids in the neighborhood a nickel for empty glass containers big enough to hold a sample of his stuff. They wash them—hopefully—then fill them with his so-called specialty. Really it's just his usual stuff with a different kind of syrup or flavoring."

"So it is possible one of the bottles would be Chanel?" Penelope asked, feeling disheartened.

Lulu leaned in with an amused look. "If that man was handed an empty bottle of Chanel, what he'd do is fill it with cheap perfume and try to pass it off to the missus—or probably one of his girlies on the side—as the real thing, that's what."

A slow smile spread Penelope's mouth, being that Lulu's suggestion did make more sense. The likelihood that Barney wasted a perfectly good bottle of empty French perfume—where would kids in his neighborhood even find something like that?—on one of his special deliveries was almost nil.

Which meant it had been delivered by someone else.

"You realize Mr. Sweeney is going to hear about this, right? Not from me of course."

Penelope twisted her lips. "Let me handle Mr. Sweeney. I can afford to speak his language these days."

"That fun old gal left you that much, huh?" Lulu asked with a grin.

She had been a frequent guest at Agnes's infamous parties. That fun old gal didn't discriminate, and not just in terms of race. It's what made her parties so notorious. Just this past summer she'd had one with a cadre of men flamboyantly dressed as women, complete with wigs and makeup and sparkling dresses. It had been an absolute snapper.

"I swear this city is like the flu the way news spreads. Yes, the fun old gal left me that much—and then some."

"Well good for you, Pen," she said with a smile. "I suppose I'll be seeing less of you now."

"Not a chance, Lulu. I plan on having more fun than ever."

Lulu laughed and lifted her glass towards Pen. "In which case, the next round is on you."

"Thanks, Lulu. As always, you're the berries."

She left, passing by the large man in front who still wasn't happy about her presence. She gave him a pert smile as she exited.

"Well?" Detective Prescott asked as she got back in the car.

"I just found another piece of the puzzle."

CHAPTER TWENTY-TWO

"CARE TO ENLIGHTEN AS TO WHAT YOU LEARNED INSIDE the Peacock Club?" Detective Prescott asked.

"One of Agnes's guests had the bottle delivered, pretending it came from...a well-known procurer of that sort of thing. I think if your detectives test the bottle, you'll find residue of whatever poison killed her. Now, I just have to narrow down the suspects."

"Well, we've got a long ride back to figure it out." He started the car while Penelope considered who the culprit might be.

"I know Raymond was back and forth into Manhattan on a regular basis. He also definitely knew who usually delivered the bottle, and probably the trademark way it was usually wrapped. He could have easily obtained an empty bottle from one of the many young women he was wooing.

"Then there's Lottie, Major Hallaway's wife. She confessed to getting bored and driving into the city this past week while she was here. And if anyone knows perfume, it's her. Though, I'm not sure if what she's wearing is Chanel. I don't know perfumes all that well. I stick to scented toilet water."

"Lavender," Detective Prescott uttered as he drove.

Penelope swiveled her head to look at him, feeling a rush of pleasure run through her. "Yes, it was my mother's favorite."

He swallowed, silently focused ahead.

Penelope smiled to herself and continued on. "It's also just as likely that it's Major Hallaway. He said he drove here from Washington, so he has his own car to use. He could have used one of his wife's empty bottles. But he seems to shy away from illegal liquor. Still, he was in army intelligence. It wouldn't be too hard to learn about who deals in illegal liquor.

"Mrs. Mayweather is the least likely suspect. I haven't noticed a scent on her, and I doubt she would have splurged on such a bottle just to empty it for these purposes. Then again, once upon a time she did have means. If she has just run out of an old bottle of perfume, it would have been the perfect container to use. And she and Agnes had become close, so she probably knew about her little gifts from—" She again stopped herself before mentioning Barney's name.

Detective Prescott chuckled but ignored it. "So, that's four people."

"Which leaves me right where I was before," Penelope said, falling back in her seat. "I *need* to narrow this down somehow."

Detective Prescott smiled. "Not so easy being a detective, after all, is it?"

Penelope turned to him feeling slightly abashed. "I apologize for that. It was unwarranted."

"Nonsense, or should I say, pineapples?"

Penelope laughed and slapped him on the arm. Why did she have such an urge to do this with a man she'd only met a few hours ago, and a police detective to boot?

"As I said, I've heard far worse. Spend enough time in the military, especially during wartime, and you might as well leave your pride behind. Soldiers are brutal with one another when it comes to verbal attacks."

"Oh, I know a few women who could probably make you hardened soldiers cry."

"Yes," he said softly as he looked ahead at the road, unsmiling. Penelope was cognizant enough to realize she had touched on something quite personal and painful. Apparently, women could be even crueler than she'd suggested.

He quickly recovered. "Come on, Detective Banks, tell me more about each of these suspects of yours."

"Actually, now that I think about it, the key might be in Agnes's room."

"Her *locked* room, correct?"

"Yes, thank you, detective," she said curtly, annoyed at his pointing out yet another pesky fact. "If I can figure out how that letter and the poison got there, then it might lead to the culprit."

"Easy as apple pie."

"Oh hush," Penelope said, but she couldn't help a short, sharp laugh.

"Okay, tell me the events that night as you know them."

"It was the same as usual, except for Chives bringing in the package of special liquor, which we know came in the bottle of Chanel."

"And if she needed anything in the middle of the night? Say, if she realized she'd been poisoned?"

Penelope's lips twisted with irritation at this problem.

"She has a call button. Yes, Beth and I checked to make sure it was working and it was. That's another puzzle to solve."

"I'll be honest Miss Banks, this is beginning to feel a lot more like a labyrinth than a puzzle."

"Except labyrinths have a way out."

"Keep going, you'll hit on something."

"So Agnes gets her usual—" she stopped, realizing now that she might be implicating more than just Agnes in criminal activity. Just because Detective Prescott had dismissed it earlier, didn't mean he wasn't filing the information away for later. She'd hate to see Chives in prison just because she said something.

"Brandy? Gin? Bourbon? It's okay to call it what it was. As I stated, not my purview."

"Golly detective, if I didn't know any better, I'd say you weren't a big fan of Prohibition."

He continued to stare ahead for a while. "I think it's caused more harm than good. Yes, I've seen alcohol become the salve for many a broken man, especially in the years after the war. However, legislating vice never ends well. It just turns people who are otherwise upstanding members of society into criminals."

Penelope thought about Cousin Cordelia and her "medicine" and laughed lightly. The thought of her as a vicious criminal was absurd. Pen didn't know what her cousin would do without her morning—

She sat up straighter, something about her cousin striking a note in her memory. Pen's mind raced back to this past week, every morning sitting at breakfast with Cousin Cordelia. Except Saturday morning there was less of her medicine than usual, which had caused her cousin to—

"I've got it!" She turned to Detective Prescott with an

excited smile. "Of course the bottle would be in her hand, don't you see?"

He turned to her with one eyebrow raised in skepticism. "You'll have to explain this one for me."

"If you were in bed and found something odd, let's say in the drawer of your nightstand, you'd pick it up out of pure curiosity, right? What is this and what is it doing in your room?"

"I suppose, but then I'd certainly call for someone, especially if I had a household full of staff at my disposal."

"One puzzle at a time. But that explains why the poison would be in her hand. She found it somewhere near her. Maybe it was in the drawer. There's a bell in there that she rings if she knows a member of the staff is close by. Perhaps when she realized the call button wasn't working for whatever reason, she opened the drawer to get the bell. Instead she finds this bottle of poison and takes hold of it, wondering what it's doing there."

"But can we assume the same about the letter? I find it hard to believe she'd encounter two strange things and hold one in each hand as she's taking her last breath? Particularly after taking the time to unfold the letter."

"They weren't necessarily in her hand, but nearby on the bed," she said weakly, noting how poor that argument was.

After casting a quick look at Penelope, Detective Prescott said, "You're getting there, keep going."

Penelope took a breath then exhaled. "Let's rewind and retrace her steps. She pours the drink, thinking it's nothing more harmless than a special blend of alcohol. Let's say she takes a sip, casually drinking as she picks up her book. So she's drinking and reading," Penelope pictured it in her head as if she was Agnes. "Drinking and reading...drinking and reading...drinking...and...reading...."

Penelope kept hitting a brick wall. The man sitting next to her wasn't helping, distraction that he was.

"Stop it," she said.

"Stop what?"

"I can tell you're itching to say something amusing or witty to make a joke of this."

He turned to her with a solemn expression. "I would never joke about death, especially murder. It's obvious that Miss Sterling meant something to you, so I'm considerate of that. Keep going, as I said, you'll get there."

She smiled in appreciation. "Okay, so...when and how do the letter and poison come in?"

"At some point all that drinking will result in the poison starting to take effect. Chief Higgins said it was arsenic, which takes a good twenty to thirty minutes to go into effect, depending on how much of it there is. The pain would hit pretty hard."

"Yes," Penelope said, nibbling her lip. "So, eventually the book drops from her hands as the poison sets in."

She thought back to the photo, the book cast aside just to the right of her.

"Wait a second! The book, it was *lying* face down, as though she placed it there to momentarily save her place. I know she hates doing that, it ruins the binding. But her bookmark was missing that night. We couldn't find it. Books, especially paperbacks, don't just happen to land open face down. She *placed* it that way. As though she encountered something else that took priority and she deliberately set it aside."

"Like a bottle of poison."

"Or a letter," Penelope said, once again getting excited. "The funny thing is, she was reading Agatha Christie. This might as well be a case in one of her books."

She gasped as the obvious practically slapped her in the face. "That's why the letter was folded! It was in the book! It must have been hidden in the pages. She set the book down to pull the letter out and unfold it, but by then it was too late. The glass in the photo was still mostly full, so there must have been so much poison that one long sip would do it."

"Arsenic doesn't have a taste or a scent, so the murderer could have put quite a bit in, enough to make it work after only a few sips."

"So that fits perfectly," Penelope said, pleased that at least something was starting to make sense.

Detective Prescott grinned at her. "Well done, Monsieur Poirot," he said, again with a perfect French accent. It made Penelope even more curious about him and his background. A Princeton grad who appreciated art, could pronounce French, and he'd obviously read Agatha Christie.

And he was a detective?

"Or Tommy and Tuppence," she said, batting her eyelashes.

"I would never take that much credit."

"Applesauce, I couldn't have figured this out without you prodding me along. You're...my muse."

He frowned, which made her laugh.

"Okay, so the letter was in the book. And the poison was, let's say in the drawer with the bell. Now we just have to figure out who put them there."

"We also have to figure out why the call button wasn't

working. Obviously someone tampered with it. Anyone tall enough could reach them in the staff area. That means either Major Hallaway or Raymond. My money is on Raymond of course."

"Hmm," Detective Prescott hummed.

"It has to be him," Penelope said, once again excited to be on the correct trail. "At first I thought it didn't make sense to bring in outside help, but now it absolutely does. He got Julia fired so he could get Edith hired. She would be able to get around the house without suspicion, using the excuse that she was performing her household duties. Agnes didn't lock her room during the day. When no one was looking, she could have planted both the poison bottle and the letter. Meanwhile Raymond could fiddle with the call service to keep it from working. He was close enough to Agnes, and heaven knows enough of a drinker to know about her special deliveries. Heck, he probably also caused the crash last year. He loves cars! Surely he'd know how to make the brakes malfunction." Now that she was on the right track, Penelope was terrifically worked up. "Ohh, I could just—!"

She stopped herself and turned to Detective Prescott with a look of embarrassment. "I mean, I would never do anything illegal of course."

He smiled as he stared ahead at the road. "I think this is definitely an avenue worth exploring, Miss Banks. You may have just helped solve this case."

"Oh, I definitely have. Those two should rot in hell for what they've done."

"Let's start with an interrogation first."

Penelope was restless the entire rest of the ride back to Glen Cove. It was dark when Detective Prescott finally parked in the drive in front, she bounded out of the car ahead of him.

The front door was opened before she could even reach it. A perfectly ashen-faced Chives looked past her toward Detective Prescott as he ascended the steps behind her.

"Oh, you're here just in time, detective. I'm afraid there has been another murder."

CHAPTER TWENTY-THREE

PENELOPE STOOD FROZEN IN PLACE AT CHIVES'S announcement that there had been another murder.

Behind her, Detective Prescott leaped into action. He came around and placed one protective hand out to keep her behind him as he confronted Chives.

"Who was killed?"

"The new maid, Edith. She's been stabbed in the neck. We aren't sure what with. She's in the hallway leading to the staff quarters."

Penelope gasped. Even Detective Prescott seemed taken aback.

"You don't say," he muttered in a terse voice.

"Yes, we've called the police already of course, but as her body was only just discovered they have yet to arrive."

"That's fine, I'll be in charge until they get here. I need everyone in the house gathered, both the guests and staff. No one has left, I trust?"

"No, sir."

"Good, do what you need to gather them all into one room. If they give you any problems, let me know. Oh, and, make sure it isn't the parlor. I would prefer them to be sober."

Chives noted with understanding then left to do the detective's bidding.

"This proves it!" Penelope hissed in a whisper. "Raymond killed her because he heard we were treating the case as a murder. No co-conspirator to rat on him. We have him!"

"I'm afraid there is no we at this point, Miss Banks. *I'll* have to handle the case from here."

"What?" Penelope's mouth fell open.

"I'm the detective with a badge. You're—"

"The one who basically handed you the suspect on a silver platter!" she argued, still in a whisper.

"And for that, I am very grateful." He said, earning himself a scowl. "But I'm afraid I need to handle it from here. Alone."

He of course had a point, as disappointing as it was. Still, Penelope couldn't help but feel sore at the idea that she'd done so much work on this only to have yet another man come in and tell her to scram.

The guests were making their way into the foyer toward the study where Chives had decided to put everyone. Benny was arm in arm with Cousin Cordelia and they approached Penelope.

"You're back," Cousin Cordelia said, looking dreadful. "Have you heard about Edith? Isn't it terrible! If it wasn't for dear Benny here, I'd be a frightful mess."

"How was the drive back?" Benny asked, arching his brow at Pen, obviously more focused on other things.

"Rather disappointing," Penelope said. She scowled at Detective Prescott, who simply offered one of his trademark subtle looks of amusement.

"Perhaps you can escort Miss Banks to the study?" Detective Prescott said to Benny.

"Surely, I'm not a suspect. I have you as the perfect alibi, don't I?" she remarked in a sardonic voice.

"Oh, does this mean we're all suspects?" Benny asked, looking positively enthralled at the prospect. "Leave it to Pen to make an otherwise dreary day exciting."

"Oh hush, Benny," she chided.

"I'll have to interview everyone who was here at the time," Detective Prescott said.

"Oh dear," Cousin Cordelia said, hand pressed to her chest with concern.

"Actually, I'm feeling rather faint. I think I'll need to retire to my bedroom instead," Penelope said, the back of her hand coming to her forehead.

Detective Prescott looked on with wry amusement.

"You don't mind, do you?" She pursed her lips. "After all, you've already interrogated me, haven't you?"

There was a loud knock at the front door. Detective Prescott answered it himself since Chives was otherwise occupied. Two officers from the Glen Cove department entered the house.

"I'm Detective Prescott, 10A precinct NYPD," he said announcing himself. "I'm here on another related case and I've already begun rounding up the guests and staff."

"I have, of course already been cleared," Penelope announced.

"Miss Banks will be joining the other guests and staff— for her own protection."

Penelope fell to the floor in a faint.

The other officers, being much more gentlemanly than Detective Prescott, jumped to her rescue.

"Are you alright, miss?"

"Here, let me help you up."

"Oh, you are too kind," Penelope said in a weak voice.

"Penelope, are you alright?" Cousin Cordelia cried, the only other member of the grouping who was fooled by her act. Benny was perfectly amused. Detective Prescott slightly less so.

"I'll be fine with some rest. Perhaps in the sitting room. I just need rest...and privacy."

With a sigh, Detective Prescott relented. "Please escort Miss Banks to the sitting room. I'll deal with her later. I'd like one of you to stay with her, just to make sure she's safe."

She frowned.

Detective Prescott smiled.

As she led the officer away to the sitting room, Penelope fumed. It seemed unfair that she should be cloistered away while the case was finalized, especially after she'd done most of the work. Granted, she hadn't factored in Edith getting killed, but surely that only proved Raymond's guilt?

The officer led her inside and closed the door behind them. After removing her coat and draping it over a chair, she paced, imagining everything that was happening elsewhere in the house. She supposed it was better to be here alone than face the venom and envy from the others. That didn't mean it wasn't frustrating just sitting here waiting.

Perhaps she should just be happy with the fact that the case was potentially solved. Agnes's murderer would be brought to justice. There was no need for her to continue being "meddlesome." Then again, it wouldn't *necessarily* be meddling if she were to simply listen in.

Penelope turned to glance at the police officer. He seemed like the accommodating sort. He'd been the quickest to reach out for her when she "fainted." He observed her with wary regard, no doubt wondering if another fainting spell was coming

"I need to use the powder room."

He stared uncertainly. "Um, I should probably escort you."

"Officer! That's rather intrusive," she replied, looking perfectly mortified. She lowered her eyelids and looked up at him from beneath her lashes, an expression of feminine bashfulness. "It's...a female issue."

His face turned red and he blinked rapidly. "I...uh... well...Miss—"

"I may be a while," she gave him a pointed look. "If that's quite alright with you?"

"Yes ma'am, er, miss, I mean—" The poor thing looked like he would have gladly traded places with the criminals he'd arrested in the past. Penelope did feel a bit badly, but surely this little bit of deception was fairly harmless.

"Thank you, officer," she said, offering a dazzling smile as she opened the door and walked out.

Penelope surreptitiously made her way to the wing of the house where the study was located. Detective Prescott had probably already singled out Raymond to interrogate first and the most likely place nearest to that was either the parlor or the library. Deciding that he would have judiciously chosen the latter, she quietly tiptoed to that closed door and pressed her ear to it. She smiled with satisfaction when she heard the muffled voices of the two men.

Raymond, the scoundrel, was already professing his ignorance about having anything to do with Edith.

"Don't be absurd. I can have any woman I want, why would I waste my time with a maid?"

"Perhaps your relationship was more professional than romantic?"

There was a pause before Raymond coughed out a sharp laugh. "Yes, I was hoping to make my living one day as a maid. She was giving me helpful advice on how the job is done," he said in a sarcastic voice before finishing with another laugh.

"I'm thinking she was helping you in a more lucrative manner."

"I didn't even know the damn woman, I'm telling you!"

"So if I were to ask the Sullivans and the Aldreds, they wouldn't have any recollection of you pleading her case for a reference?"

"That's..." there was a long pause. "Don't be ridiculous." His voice was far less certain now.

"Mr. Colley." Detective Prescott's voice was so firm and commanding even Penelope became tense. "This is not a simple inquiry into some silly dalliance between you and the maid. This is a murder investigation, and right now you are the most likely suspect. This means, at best, life in prison, sir. *Life.* Now I suggest you start pleading your case as to why I shouldn't arrest you right now and be done with it, and stop denying that you even knew the woman. Because I do have a witness that will claim otherwise."

Penelope smiled with satisfaction, imagining Raymond's look of shock at that revelation.

"Alright, you've found me out. I was getting it on with the maid. Happy?"

"No."

"What do you want from me? I didn't kill Edith! Why the hell would I?" Raymond cried.

"Because she was your partner in crime. What was it, Mr. Colley? Did she threaten to give you up to the police? Reveal your little scheme?"

"What scheme?" Raymond practically yelled.

"Fine, keep denying it. Right now, I have you confessing to a romantic relationship with the victim, who has been employed here less than a week. I have multiple, quite prominent, families who will attest to you creating a situation for her, conveniently enough the same week your Aunt —from whom you no doubt expected to receive a rather large inheritance—was murdered." Raymond must have reacted to that because Detective Prescott went on to say, "Oh yes, Mr. Colley, we are officially declaring Miss Sterling's death a murder. Which makes two victims, both of whom you had more reason than anyone to murder—"

"Stop! Just—just stop it, now!" Raymond shouted, his voice panicky. "I didn't kill Aunt Agnes! I didn't even get that much from her, certainly not enough to live on."

"But you didn't know that before she died."

"Okay, yeah but still, I had no reason to kill her. Hell, out of all of those others, I had the least reason to. Penelope was the one who got the lion's share of the kale. Why isn't she in here right now?"

"Miss Banks has an alibi for that night."

"Does she?" Raymond asked in a skeptical tone. "Well how convenient for her."

"But not for you, since that still leaves you as the number one suspect."

"What about that major and Lottie? He's a relative and she's a damn expensive trinket if you know what I mean."

"I'm focused on Edith right now, Mr. Colley. Frankly, I'm happy to let Glen Cove handle Miss Sterling's death. But Edith? That case practically solves itself. You might as well be holding the weapon in your hand right now."

Penelope frowned. Was this just another ploy or did he really not care about Agnes's murder case?

"I didn't kill her! Why would I?"

"You keep saying that. Do you need me to answer the question for you? One, you were the one who knew her longer and, frankly, more intimately than anyone here at the time. Two, you were seen arguing with her recently."

"What?" Raymond asked in surprise.

Detective Prescott continued.

"You were also the one to situate her here in the first place. I'll bet if I look into her history, there will be no record of any employment as a maid. In fact, I'll bet I'd find something rather unsavory. Frankly, unless you can convince me otherwise, I'm ready to slap the cuffs on you and haul you down—"

"I didn't kill her! I swear it! Hell, I had every reason to want her alive, especially now!"

"Not good enough, Mr. Colley. I certainly hope you have enough money for a good attorney because—"

"Wait, wait just a minute!" Raymond sounded as though he were crying in frustration right now. Gone was the self-assured cake-eater, in his place was a scared little boy.

"Tick tock, Mr. Raymond. My patience will only last so long."

"Okay, Edith is—was...she wasn't a maid."

"Tell me something I don't already know."

"She...may have...been involved in...a little bit of forgery."

After a long pause, Detective Prescott spoke up. "Continue."

"I mean, that's it. I had no idea, not until after I'd taken pity on her and gotten her hired."

"That sounds like a motive for murder to me, Mr. Colley. I do believe you've just made my case."

"Wait! What the hell do you mean?"

"I mean, you're going down for her murder unless you give me a good reason why you had no reason to kill her."

"But...come on!"

"I'm not in the business of coming on. I'm in the business of arresting murderers."

"Okay fine! I knew, alright? I knew what she was. That's why when Julia suddenly got fired for the theft, I figured it was the perfect opportunity to bring Edith in."

"So...you didn't frame Julia for the theft," the detective confirmed.

"No way are you pinning that one on me. Julia stole those earrings. I had nothing to do with that!"

There was a long pause. No doubt Detective Prescott was suffering the same bit of surprise that Penelope was. Julia's supposed theft was nothing more than a coincidence? That didn't make any sense.

Raymond continued on, not realizing he had just implanted a seed of doubt in his accusers. "Anyway, Edith had already, um, handled paintings at other homes. She didn't want it tied back to me by targeting Agnes's stuff, which would have been more convenient if you ask me. I finally persuaded her to do the Matisse. When no one even noticed, I thought, why not do more?"

"When was the Matisse replaced with a fake?"

"When Agnes was in Manhattan for her New Year's Eve party."

"Okay, go on."

Penelope stood up straighter, realizing what was happening. Detective Prescott was only working on his case regarding the painting and had been during this entire interrogation. He didn't care about Edith's death, or Agnes's for that matter!

She almost made the grave mistake of grabbing the doorknob and opening it in her rush to accuse him. But there would be time for that later. Raymond had just confessed to being in cahoots with Edith, the maestra who could recreate the work of others—sometimes with her additional own cheeky touches. No wonder Raymond had been so mad at her that night after discovering the mouse-or-rat on the Matisse.

"So you see, why would I kill her? Agnes only left me ten thousand dollars. At least with Edith around, we could have made money from other paintings. With her dead, I'm in a fine mess, aren't I?"

"My heart goes out to you."

"Yeah, yeah, scoff all you want. You're just a detective, making what? A few hundred a week?"

Detective Prescott coughed out a laugh. Penelope had to keep from coughing out one of her own. The wealthy really were clueless about the average person's income.

"Whatever. You wouldn't understand. I have needs, and ten thousand sure as hell isn't going to cover them. At least with Edith alive, I could...well, you know?"

"Make more than a few hundred a week?"

"Yeah. I'd at least be able to cover my debts and maybe avoid living like an animal scrounging for scraps."

"Let's say I believe you didn't kill Edith. That still doesn't clear you for Agnes's death. After all, you didn't know she was only going to leave you the *paltry* sum of ten thousand dollars." She could hear the sarcasm in his voice.

Penelope exhaled with satisfaction. He was taking her murder seriously.

"Again, why would I kill Agnes? At least I was getting an allowance from her, and with Edith here we had unfettered access to more paintings. With both of them dead it means both sources of income are now gone."

"You could have potentially received a lot more upon Agnes's death."

"Not likely," Raymond muttered in a disgruntled tone. "She knew my debts were being called in from places all over town. Every damn day I got another talking-to from her about how much I was spending on clothes, or restaurants, or other places I frequented. That's why I've spent so much time out here lately. I was trying to...make a better impression with her." He exhaled a sardonic laugh. "I sure as hell wasn't the only one. You should be looking at those other vultures out there. I wasn't even here that night."

"You sure about that? And before you answer, keep in mind I have witnesses."

"Okay, yes, I came in late that night. Arabella, the cook will confirm it. I had to sit and listen to her blather on as she fed me. I had meant to meet up with Edith in order to— never mind, but she certainly ruined those plans. I went to bed after that. I swear!"

Penelope realized that the interrogation was coming to an end. Raymond was responsible for the paintings, but not the murders, at least as far as Detective Prescott was concerned.

She was reluctant to go back and twiddle her thumbs in the sitting room. Right now, she essentially had the house to herself. It was the perfect opportunity to learn more about one of the stickier problems eluding her in solving Agnes's murder.

Penelope quietly stepped away and headed to the staff area.

CHAPTER TWENTY-FOUR

The bells.

Or rather, the lighted buzzing system that alerted staff that one of the guests needed tending to. Each place was marked with a different room in the house, a label indicating which guest was staying in which room. Penelope focused on the first one along the row: Agnes's suite.

To the casual eye there appeared to be nothing wrong with it. Beth had assured Penelope that it had been working that night.

Only a handful of people could even reach it, namely Raymond and Major Hallaway. The former had perhaps been cleared. That left the major.

Penelope wished there was some way to get a closer look. Perhaps a ladder or—

Her eyes landed on the doorway to the kitchen. The stepping stool!

She rushed over and grabbed it, bringing it to the row of buzzers. Using the stool she could easily reach them, getting a close enough look to see if anything had been fiddled with.

This of course meant that any of the guests could have reached it. But scanning the wires and the buzzer itself, there was no hint whatsoever of tampering.

Perhaps all the staff had simply slept through the noise? But what murderer would rely on that hope?

"Ugh!" Penelope exclaimed, banging her fist against the wall below it. It jostled the row of buzzers enough for her to note that one of them was slightly loosened.

Penelope peered closer at the third one, which had shaken a bit. She flicked it with her finger and it moved again. Fiddling with it some more she discovered that it was simply twisted onto a casing holding it in place. She rotated it enough to remove it. While there was no wiring inside, she could see how it worked. It was like a light bulb, it had to be placed flush against the backing, otherwise there was no connection for the electricity. If it was too loose, it no doubt wouldn't make a noise or light up at all.

Feeling her heart beat a bit faster, Penelope screwed it back on and tried the one for Agnes's suite. It was securely tightened so much that she had to struggle to twist it off.

"Pineapples!" she said, frustrated. She twisted it back on, making sure it was secure.

She studied the row for a moment, wondering what she had missed. Just to be sure, she checked the second in line. It was securely screwed, but not as tight as Agnes's had been. With sudden dawning, she tried the others. They were all secured to various degrees, enough for them to work, but not so much one would think they had recently been securely tightened.

As Agnes's had been.

So, perhaps someone had loosened it just enough that it wouldn't work, then later on, after Agnes was dead, tightened it again, making sure it was as secure as possible to avoid suspicion.

With a smile of satisfaction at discovering one more *how*, even if the *who* still eluded her, Penelope quickly walked back to the main part of the house.

She was just in time to run into both Detective Prescott leading a now handcuffed Raymond Colley away, and the annoyed police officer who was supposed to be watching her.

"Miss Banks, why am I not surprised to find you anywhere other than where you're supposed to be?" Detective Prescott said in a testy voice.

"I've just figured something out!"

"Despite my warning to leave it to me."

"It's a clue," she continued. "I know how the killer disrupted the call service."

"You didn't tamper with it did you?"

"Well..." She hadn't really thought of that but could see how he might be upset about that. "I mean yes, but—"

"Miss Banks," he sighed, briefly closing his eyes. He turned to the other police officer. "Can you *please* escort her to the *study* with everyone else, and keep watch to *make sure* she doesn't leave."

At this point, arguing was pointless. In fact, being in the same room as the other suspects worked perfectly for her purposes. It was the optimal situation to do a bit more interrogating. She didn't resist when the disgruntled officer led her there and made sure to close the door behind her.

In the large study, all eyes turned to the newest arrival. The staff had segregated themselves to one side of the room. She saw Benny with Cousin Cordelia and Mrs. Mayweather comfortably seated together on the couch chattering away. Major Hallaway and his wife were in a corner, huddled together in private conversation.

They were the only two she hadn't been able to learn more about beyond what she'd discovered from the will and Agnes's letter. She decided to focus on them first.

She walked over and approached them. Before they could so much as note her presence she began talking.

"Such a tragedy isn't it? Why would anyone kill Edith?" Penelope asked as she pulled a chair closer and sat down.

Neither of them seemed pleased at the intrusion into their quiet little tête-à-tête. Lottie glared at her, but the major seemed rather shaken.

"Yes, it is quite unfortunate. My wife and I were just discussing it."

"I just can't understand why anyone would want her dead. She's a maid, one who'd only been here less than a week in fact," Penelope said.

"Maybe someone didn't like the way she turned down the bed," Lottie said in a dry voice, still giving Penelope the evil eye.

"Lottie, that is hardly appropriate," her husband scolded.

"People react to tragedies in strange ways," Penelope said, swallowing her disdain. "Speaking of which, I can't help but think about Agnes, most notably her will."

That had both of them sporting looks of cautious interest.

"I still plan on hiring an attorney. There is something very strange about leaving so much to one individual and such a meager sum to her own cousin," Major Hallaway said.

"I agree."

Now they both looked perfectly stunned.

"I can't help but feel slightly guilty about the imbalance in the distribution of her estate. After all, you were her family."

"Yeah, he was," Lottie spat.

Penelope ignored that as she continued. Her conversation with Mrs. Mayweather earlier today had been helpful. She could swallow her contempt long enough to use it now. "Perhaps she thought you weren't in need of her money?" Her eyes briefly darted to Lottie, who at some point had changed out of the modest black dress and into a fiery red number, accentuated with her pearls again, today there was also a ruby ring to match.

"What are you implying?" Major Hallaway asked with an indignant look.

Lottie didn't look fooled at all. "She's sayin' we put on too many airs is what."

Penelope realized that while the Major was satisfied continuing his facade of ignorance and pride, Lottie had no such qualms. Frankly, she preferred his wife's transparency.

"I'm doing no such thing. There is nothing wrong with wearing fine clothes and jewelry. I'm only trying to look at this from Agnes's point of view. I know many people who still hold onto sentimental pieces even though they may not *currently* be flush with money."

"Our financial circumstances are none of your business," Major Hallaway blustered. "Past or present."

"Hold on, lovey," Lottie said, possessively stroking her necklace. "Are you offering us some of your dough?"

"How much would you need?"

"We don't need anything, thank you very much! As I said, our finances are our business, and none of yours. How my wife gets her jewelry is also none of your business."

Penelope stared at him, realizing something he'd said

seemed odd. Was he implying that he wasn't the one buying the jewelry for her? So where was she "getting" it? Pen didn't know much about military salaries, but she did know a bit about the cost of jewelry and furs.

Something Benny had suggested struck her and she gasped in shock. Was Lottie a kept woman, getting the jewelry from men she had been seeing outside of her marriage? If so, Major Hallaway was awfully unbothered about the whole affair, as much as Lottie liked to flash her gifts.

No, that couldn't be it. A man as prideful as Major Hallaway wouldn't allow it. He was also quite patronizing when it came to her other vices like drinking or talking out of turn. Or wearing too much perfume.

"I was curious about that scent of yours. What brand of perfume is it?"

Lottie studied her with a brow furrowed in confusion, no doubt at the detour this conversation was taking.

"Shalimar. It's my signature scent. I heard that some-where, and I think it's fitting. My signature." She slid her eyes to Major Hallaway, who seemed a bit more mollified at the change in subjects. "A gift from this one. He eventually got it right."

"An expensive endeavor," he groused.

Shalimar, not Chanel No. 5.

In retrospect, it wasn't a huge surprise. Lottie wouldn't be dumb enough to use the same bottle of the scent she wore. And Major Hallaway wouldn't have stooped to something so blatantly feminine in order to kill Agnes. And how would they even know about Barney's special delivery?

The jewelry still nagged at Penelope. How would a woman in a marriage to a man of comfortable, but certainly not abundant means get so much expensive jewelry? A man who had to beg Agnes for a loan?

She rewound the past few days in her head to see if anything stood out. It came to her gradually this time, piecing several things together. Mostly, it was something Beth had said about how she thought Agnes should keep her door locked when she wasn't in.

"One moment," Penelope said. The two of them started in surprise as she shot up from her chair and walked away.

Penelope headed straight toward Chives.

"Can I speak with you a moment?"

He promptly stood and nodded. "Of course Miss Banks."

Penelope drew him into a private corner. "Has anything gone missing this week? I mean, beyond the earrings Julia supposedly stole?"

He demurred for just a moment. "I didn't want to say anything, as I have no definitive proof as to who has taken it, but yes, several pieces of silverware."

The same ones Lottie had pointed out at dinner were worth quite a bit.

"I see. And, did anything go missing during the weeks before Agnes's accident?"

He coughed softly and swallowed. "Miss Sterling asked that I not speak of it. She preferred not to create a fuss over it, mostly because we never had proof of who the culprit was."

"But..."

"Yes, a ruby ring. Miss Sterling never wore it. I don't even remember what it looked like, but it had sentimental value to her all the same."

"Why that little..." Penelope stopped herself, tempering her anger. No wonder Agnes left the major and his wife so little in the will. It seemed Lottie was capable of fending for herself quite well.

"Thank you, Chives," Penelope said, heading back to the Hallaways.

As she approached, she added up all the evidence. Both of them knew how to drive, which meant they knew about cars. They had both conveniently been here right before Agnes's accident. They also had the means and opportunity to escape into town to have a bottle delivered. Lottie had mentioned something about her days in New York and knowing "where to get the best booze in town." Surely she knew about Barney. Both were certainly familiar with perfume. The major had indicated that he'd bought her several before she finally settled on Shalimar. Perhaps Chanel had been one of his misses?

Then there was the letter Major Hallaway claimed to have received inviting him to stay here. It could have easily been forged...with the same hand that had forged Agnes's suicide note. After all Major Hallaway had worked with Army intelligence, surely he knew a thing or two about doctoring documents.

And both certainly had motive.

Major Hallaway had been denied another loan from Agnes.

Lottie had perhaps grown tired of stealing here and there and decided to go for the entire cache of Agnes's money.

As for Edith, well, perhaps she had learned what they had done and needed to be eliminated. That was something she could focus on later. For now, Penelope had at least enough to point the finger at wrongdoing.

Starting with one piece of jewelry in particular.

"Where did you get that ring?" she asked as she sat down with them again.

"I beg your pardon?" Major Hallaway asked.

Lottie simply stared at Penelope, a cool look on her face.

"Agnes gave it to me. A gift."

Penelope didn't bother responding, simply narrowing her gaze with contempt instead.

"Lottie, you didn't!" Major Hallaway gasped, turning to his wife.

Penelope felt her heart stop. Was he actually accusing his wife of murder right in front of her?

Lottie slid her eyes to her husband, a smug look on her face. "She wasn't usin' it. A perfectly nice ring just hidden away in the back of some drawer and—"

"Stop it, stop it right now." Penelope was surprised at how resigned her husband's voice was, frustration and disappointment coloring every word. "This is exactly why we had to leave, start over in Washington D.C."

"I don't see what the problem is. She's dead, she won't even care."

"I can't believe you!" Penelope gasped. "You murder her and then have the gall to flaunt the jewelry you stole?"

"Murder?" Lottie repeated, turning her attention back to Penelope in surprise. She coughed out a laugh. "I didn't murder anyone."

"Miss Banks," Major Hallaway said in a low, patient tone. "My wife, she...has a problem. She has a compulsion to take things, expensive things. We have been working on it. Yes, I've struggled to clean up her minor transgressions. But she's hardly a murderer. Neither am I."

"Of course you'd say that."

He exhaled a soft, sardonic laugh. "We had no reason to kill Agnes."

"It's funny, everyone seems to be claiming that these days."

"Except you," Lottie sneered. "You certainly made out okay, didn't you?"

Major Hallaway rested his hand on hers to silence her. "This isn't helping, Loretta."

He turned his attention back to Penelope. "We had no reason to want Agnes dead, and there's someone who can back that statement up as a witness."

Penelope felt her heart sink but held her breath until it was revealed.

"Julia," Lottie muttered, twisting her lips with annoyance. "The maid."

It took a second for Penelope to understand. "Was it you who framed her?"

Lottie simply lifted her chin defiantly.

"I didn't find out until after the fact. When I saw my wife had, er, *inadvertently* taken Mrs. Mayweather's earrings, I insisted she return them."

Penelope kept from making a noise of disbelief that the theft was "inadvertent."

"I thought Agnes inviting us here meant...well, never mind that. I knew if she learned about the theft it might ruin things for us. But when Agnes finally sat us down and told us she wouldn't give us a single cent even in her will, it didn't matter. Julia was there to overhear it, which is why I suppose my wife decided to punish her in a way." He turned to give Lottie a censuring look.

"What?" Lottie shrugged. "That's what the little sneak deserved for snooping."

"Obviously we both feel bad about that," Major Hallaway said through gritted teeth. Penelope gave him an incredulous look. "All the same, if the authorities need proof that we had no reason to want Agnes dead, they can talk to her and she can confirm what she overheard. Agnes was cutting us off for good, even after her death. Frankly, we were surprised to get the ten thousand dollars. I suppose in the end she decided something was better than nothing for family."

"You seemed pretty heated this morning."

"That was, well to be honest, when I saw how much that awful nephew of hers received, it felt like a slight. Then when I heard how much you were to get, well, I couldn't understand why she'd be so generous with someone who wasn't family. Yes, I confess I was rather put out by that. Perhaps there was a bit of envy as well. It was an overreaction, that's all. As I said, even the ten thousand dollars is more than we expected."

Lottie leaned in with a cool smirk. "Face it, *Pen*, if you're looking for a murderer, we ain't it, and you ain't no Agatha Christie."

Despite her contempt for both of them, they had certainly filled in the blanks well enough. It wouldn't be difficult to find poor Julia and confirm what they had stated. If Agnes had told them in no uncertain terms that they were not receiving anything even after her death, why kill her? Didn't it make more sense to try and worm their way back into her good graces first?

Lottie was a thief, and Major Hallaway cleaned up her messes. Hardly innocent, but not necessarily murderers.

Which left one person remaining as a suspect.

Penelope turned to look at Mrs. Mayweather, innocently smiling at something Benny was telling her.

Was it all a facade?

CHAPTER TWENTY-FIVE

PENELOPE ESCAPED TO A SOLITARY CORNER OF THE study to think. It was becoming exceedingly obvious that jumping to conclusions too soon was the wrong approach. Yes, it had resulted in various *other* crimes being uncovered, but that got her no closer to finding proof of Agnes's murder.

Detective Prescott was right, this wasn't so easy.

Frankly, playing cards was far less difficult. Cards made sense, they were orderly and made sense. Human nature was a far different animal.

At this point, she could have left it to the Glen Cove police to solve, being that they were now treating Agnes's death as a murder. However, Agnes had been right in her assessment in the letter. Penelope wasn't one to let a puzzle go unsolved.

There had to be proof that Mrs. Mayweather was the murderer, she just had to figure out how to find it. The woman had proven herself to be a talker, but she had also shown an ability to have a ready answer for any questions that might expose her.

Thus, Penelope would have to try a different method of procuring information. She thought about what she knew of the woman, her past and present, specifically with regard to her relationship with Agnes.

The letters!

Mrs. Mayweather had mentioned bringing them here, presumably to revisit and reminisce with Agnes. They were up in her room, and Penelope was sure that the police would find they were a perfect match to the letter Agnes had supposedly written up her death note. After all, they had both learned their penmanship from the same school.

There was a second exit from the study that wasn't guarded. Penelope ignored the various looks from everyone as she made her way to that door to leave. She cautiously opened it to make sure there was no officer on the other side, then left.

She had seen Cousin Cordelia head to Mrs. Mayweather's room earlier today, so she knew which was hers. Pen quietly made her way up the stairs, which were blessedly out of view of where the officer stood watch.

Once on the landing, a new and sudden thought occurred to Penelope that had her stopping in her tracks. A slow and steady smile spread her mouth when she fully realized what it was.

She hurried on. If she found what she was looking for, it would be even better proof than the letters.

Penelope silently opened the door to the bedroom. She took a moment to look around deciding where to start. Pen began with her personal effects.

It took her several minutes of searching, going through the wardrobe, dresser drawers, nightstand, even under the bed. She finally found what she was looking for after a more thorough search had her standing on a chair to feel along the top of the wardrobe. Her hands landed on, among other things, the bookmark she had given Agnes for Christmas.

"Got it," Penelope said with satisfaction. It had been quickly wiped clean, but she could still see a tiny bit of blood in the feathers of the peacock.

"Congratulations," a voice said from the door.

Penelope spun around to face Lottie Hallaway.

She considered Penelope with an assessing look as she quietly closed the door behind her. "It was the Agatha Christie thing wasn't it?"

"You did mention last night that you weren't a reader. Only someone who read books, specifically mysteries would even know who she was. I guess you saw it on Agnes's nightstand?"

Lottie breathed out a soft laugh. "Oops!"

"It all adds up in retrospect. You being here right before her accident last year. Your husband tried to keep you quiet about that one, didn't he? Is he in on this?"

"Lovey?" She laughed. "He thinks I'm an angel—well, besides the stealing thing. He just didn't want you knowing he was askin' Agnes for money last time we were here. He's sensitive about that kind of thing."

"I suppose he knows nothing about the perfume either," Penelope said, still skeptical. "How did you know Barney was the one to send her liquor?"

"I'm a pretty good listener. You'd be surprised the things you overhear when people think you're nothing more than a dimwitted trollop. Raymond has a loose mouth, especially when he's blotto. But he has nothing on that Iris Mayweather. Last time we was here, she wouldn't shut up about those letters Agnes sent. I knew she kept them in her room when she came over, which was all the time for Pete's sake. That alone shoulda convinced someone Agnes wanted to commit suicide. I certainly did every time she opened her mouth. Anyway, I copied the handwriting then, figuring it would come in handy eventually. It was easy enough to get everything into her room during the day when no one was around. The fact that she locked her doors at night while she slept was the beauty of it all."

"And the car last year? I suppose that was you as well?"

"Lovey taught me everything about cars. As much as he hated me driving around town on my own, he also didn't want nothin' to happen to me while I was out. He's sweet that way. I guess it kinda came in handy, didn't it?" She grinned.

"Why kill Agnes?" Penelope asked, caring more about that than anything.

Lottie shrugged, coming closer. "Yeah sure, she said we weren't gettin' nothing, but I knew we could contest the will. I've seen it done before—successfully. Rich people always get what they want. Frankly, so do I. Lovey wanted to wait and cozy up to her, see if she would budge. I was tired of waiting."

She came closer, and Penelope backed up, realizing she was cornered on the other side of the room by the bed.

"I suppose Edith found out what you'd done. Is that why you killed her with this?"

Lottie smirked. "The little minx has a nose for digging up secrets. I suppose it takes a thief to know another. I guess by now I'm a bona fide expert at killing, aren't I? What's one more?"

Penelope backed up. She was in the corner between the bed and the window with no means of escape. Best to distract her somehow.

So she laughed.

Lottie paused, a confused look coming to her face.

"You just couldn't help yourself, could you?" Penelope said, lifting the bookmark. "Agnes wasn't one for showy displays of wealth. She didn't own much jewelry or fine things. That's why she never even wore that ring you stole. When you saw this, you probably thought it was worth something, didn't you?"

Lottie frowned.

"I would have thought an experienced thief such as yourself would have a better eye for such things. It's not gold, not fully. It's gold-plated over metal, you see. An understandable mistake, after all, why would Agnes have anything but the best? It was a gift, from me. I wasn't quite as flush with kale as that fun old bird. That's why she appreciated it and used it. A woman who has everything? She prefers a different kind of wealth. You no doubt stole it while you were planting the letter. A stupid move."

Lottie scowled at her. "Doesn't matter now. I've already tried suicide and stabbing. Guess I'll have to make your death look like an accident."

As Lottie raced toward her, Penelope struck inspiration, reaching out to press the call button on the nightstand next to her. It was only when Lottie was on her, trying to wrestle away the bookmark, that she realized everyone was still in the study, far away from the staff area.

Fighting Lottie off was like wrestling with a tiger, all claws and snarling mouth. She had Penelope pinned down on the bed. At this point, Pen was screaming, hoping someone would at least hear her despite how big the house was.

Lottie was relentless. She managed to pry the bookmark from Penelope's hand. Her idea about making this look like an accident was apparently dismissed in the fury that overtook her. Penelope froze as Lottie's arm rose in the air, the bookmark directed toward her, pointed end aimed right for her throat.

It was only when Lottie was pulled away from her that she realized they weren't alone. Lottie was still as rabid as a wild animal as Detective Prescott held onto her. She was no match for the detective who had her in a strong grip.

"Miss Banks, are you alright?" Chives said, quickly coming to her aide.

"You heard the call button?" Penelope gasped in surprise, sitting up.

"I saw Miss Hallaway follow you out, Miss Banks. I knew she must have been up to something. The detective here was kind enough to join me."

Penelope could have hugged Chives.

She had more sordid ideas about the detective.

Detective Prescott grinned at her as he easily held the still raging Lottie in his grip. "I should have you arrested for interfering with an investigation. Still, congratulations Detective Banks, it seems you've finally solved a case."

CHAPTER TWENTY-SIX

LATER THAT WEEK

"WELL THAT WAS A LOVELY SERVICE," COUSIN
Cordelia said as Leonard drove them into Manhattan from
Long Island where Agnes Sterling had finally been laid to
rest.

"Despite the crowds and worse, the press," Penelope
grumbled.

Two murders and a controversial will were enough to
draw a crowd to Agnes's funeral. If it hadn't been for the
Glen Cove police—with whom Penelope now had a *some-what* cordial relationship, being that the officer who had
sold Agnes's photos to Freddy Manchin had been
summarily fired—it would have been a perfect circus.

Leonard parked in front of their old apartment building.
Even though Agnes had left him and other members of the
staff enough to quit working at least for a good while, he'd
asked to stay on with her, mostly because all the cars were
now hers.

*"Where else am I going to have access to such quality
driving machines?"*

Penelope was more than grateful, being that she'd never learned to drive herself.

Both Chives and Arabella had also begged to stay on in her service as well, which made her even more grateful. It seemed the transition back to her old life would be fairly seamless. She wondered what her father would think about that.

"I'm going to miss this apartment," she said as Leonard opened the car door for them. She exited and stared up at the building that had been her home for the past three years. She turned to Cousin Cordelia. "You're still happy about the move, aren't you?"

Cousin Cordelia sighed. "I must admit, I do have fond memories with Harold here, but it *would* be nice to have a bit more space."

That was an understatement. Agnes's apartment facing Central Park was huge.

"Change can sometimes be a good thing," Penelope said, squeezing her cousin's arm as she led her up the steps to the front door. She realized with a bittersweet feeling that her late nights sneaking up these steps were at an end. Even arriving back home from a long day working for Mr. Brown —to whom she had enthusiastically given her notice— conjured up a bit of nostalgia.

Still, she was looking forward to the future, all the same. Already she had ideas about what she would do with it— something for which she also had Agnes to thank.

Penelope and Cousin Cordelia weren't the only ones facing change.

Penelope had agreed to buy Mrs. Mayweather a quaint but lovely little house in Massachusetts near the sea. Cousin Cordelia was already planning her visits.

Raymond Colley was facing a hefty sentence for his

participation in Edith's forgery and theft. It came as no surprise to Penelope that several wealthy young ladies had enthusiastically provided the means by which he could hire the best attorney money could buy. That was one trial that would make the society pages. Raymond Colley was still quite popular among the young socialites.

Lottie Hallaway's trial would be no less sensationalized. However, she had only one champion standing by her. The police had found quite the pile of loot she'd stolen over the years, a lot of it quietly cleaned up by her husband—and much of it not. Major Hallaway truly was a fool in love, even when the crimes of his wife were glaring and undisputed.

Penelope felt Julia was owed compensation for her troubles and added more to the amount Agnes had left her in the trust. That, along with the clearing of her good name, would hopefully make up for how terribly she'd been wronged.

Penelope was happy to put that entire episode behind her. She wouldn't ruin her memories of Agnes with those terrible few days in Long Island. Thanks to her old friend, she now had options in life.

She also had Agnes to thank for introducing her to a certain someone who wasn't *entirely* terrible. She smiled thinking about the offhanded remark she had made to her father about Agnes leaving her a husband in her will.

Not that Penelope was entertaining any ideas about getting married.

Yet.

Cousin Cordelia and Penelope entered the apartment... and found their maid Sarah passed out on the sofa.

"Heavens, is she dead?" Cousin Cordelia exclaimed in horror.

They both rushed over to the sofa.

"I think she's completely zozzled," Penelope said with a laugh, noting the now empty bottle of medicinal brandy she had splurged on only last weekend.

"My medicine!" Cousin Cordelia cried.

"I'm pretty sure she drank it all. No wonder she's completely out," Penelope said. "At least now we know why it went so fast. She's probably been nipping a bit here and there for some time now."

"Oh, the little devil! When she wakes up I fully plan on terminating her service! What ever am I to do now?"

Penelope refrained from laughing at the absurdity of it all. Instead, she hooked her arm through her cousin's. "Let's have champagne instead—in Agnes's honor. I know a place."

EPILOGUE

"Miss Banks," Chives announced. "There is a Detective Prescott to see you."

It hadn't taken long for Penelope and Cousin Cordelia to move into Agnes's 5th Avenue apartment. It helped that it was already furnished. She was very much getting used to being a millionaire but certainly didn't plan on remaining idle. Already she was making plans about her next venture in life.

"Of course," she said, perking up at the surprise announcement.

Penelope wasn't sure what had earned her a visit. The last time she had seen him had been at Agnes's funeral, but he had maintained a professional stance with her then, which was somewhat of a disappointment.

He entered and she felt her breath quicken at the sight of him.

"To what do I owe the pleasure?" she asked with a coy smile as she gestured to the chair across from her in the living room.

He held up a large envelope. "A gift, courtesy of one Freddy Manchin."

"You got them!" she exclaimed, sitting up straighter. She was ashamed to admit to herself that, with the funeral and the move, she had been so busy she'd forgotten about the unfortunate photos.

He smiled and handed them to her. She stood up to meet him rather than remain seated.

"You didn't...do anything terrible to him to get these did you?"

He grinned. "Don't worry. I'm not that kind of cop. He's still very much in one piece."

She smiled, even though she would have happily wrung the man's neck herself.

"So, it seems you've settled in nicely," he said, looking around.

"I am very fortunate."

"And no doubt quite popular. How many offers of marriage have you had so far?"

Penelope wasn't sure if he was asking out of personal interest but the idea pleased her.

"Why in the world would I want to get married? As Jane Austen very correctly pointed out, *men* are the ones in want of a wife. And why not? It's a perfectly satisfactory situation for them. They have someone to give them children, take care of them when they're sick, maintain their homes, and," she paused and arched one eyebrow at him, "other endeavors."

"Other endeavors?"

"Yes, endeavors that I also have no interest in," she scoffed, though her mouth pursed with amusement.

"Hmm, that's a shame, I've heard that *certain* endeavors can be quite enjoyable."

"I suppose that depends on who one is...*endeavoring* with."

"Indeed," he replied with a solemn nod.

"Have you endeavored with anyone?"

"What a question," he said, looking so highly offended she knew he must be teasing and she laughed. "And you, Miss Banks?"

She tilted her head and grinned. "What a question, Detective Prescott!"

He laughed. "That was rather unprofessional of me, wasn't it?"

"It very much was," she said tartly, but with a smile. "But, speaking of professions, you might as well be the first to know which one I plan on taking up."

"What would that be?"

"I'm surprised you need to ask. After all, you yourself said I was a good detective."

His brows knitted together with wariness. "Oh no."

"Oh yes," she retorted, glaring at him. "I plan on becoming a private detective. Services for those who aren't taken seriously by the police or anyone else."

He laughed softly. "I pity the criminals of New York."

Penelope smiled at the compliment.

"And the police detectives of New York."

She frowned, which made him laugh.

"Don't be sore, Miss Banks. I think most of them will certainly come to appreciate you, once they get past your stubborn nature...your uncensored tongue...your complete disregard for your own safety..."

"If you're just going to insult me—"

He laughed. "No, I truly think it might be your calling in life, Miss Banks. I have no doubt you'll do well at it. After all, you've already solved one big case."

"Thank you, detective. I suppose this means we'll be seeing more of each other now." A thought which sent a decided thrill of anticipation through her. He himself was still a bit of a mystery to her, one she wouldn't mind unraveling little by little.

Detective Prescott considered her with an enigmatic smile. "I very much look forward to that, Miss Banks."

Continue on For Your Free Book!

GET YOUR FREE BOOK!

Mischief at The Peacock Club

**A bold theft at the infamous Peacock Club.
Can Penelope solve it to save her own neck?**

1924 New York

Penelope "Pen" Banks has spent the past two years making ends meet by playing cards. It's another Saturday night at The Peacock Club, one of her favorite haunts, and she has her sites set on a big fish, who just happens to be the special guest of the infamous Jack Sweeney.

After inducing Rupert Cartland, into a game of cards, Pen thinks it just might be her lucky night. Unfortunately, before the night ends, Rupert has been robbed—his diamond cuff links, ruby pinky ring, gold watch, and wallet...all gone!

With The Peacock Club's reputation on the line, Mr. Sweeney, aided by the heavy hand of his chief underling Tommy Callahan, is holding everyone captive until the culprit is found.

For the promise of a nice payoff, not to mention escaping the club in one piece, Penelope Banks is willing to put her unique mind to work to find out just who stole the goods.

This is a prequel novella to the *Penelope Banks Murder Mysteries* series, taking place at The Peacock Club before Penelope Banks became a private investigator.

Access your book at the link below:
https://dl.bookfunnel.com/4sv9fir4h3

ALSO BY COLETTE CLARK

ABOUT THE AUTHOR

Colette Clark lives in New York and has always enjoyed learning more about the history of her amazing city. She decided to combine that curiosity and love of learning with her addiction to reading and watching mysteries. Her first series, **Penelope Banks Murder Mysteries** is the result of those passions. When she's not writing she can be found doing Sudoku puzzles, drawing, eating tacos, visiting museums dedicated to unusual/weird/wacky things, and, of course, reading mysteries by other great authors.

Join my Newsletter to receive news about New Releases and Sales!
https://dashboard.mailerlite.com/forms/148684/726783564877673 18/share